A Forbidden
Love

A Short Novel

KEITH ALBRECHT

ISBN 978-1-0980-2676-9 (paperback)
ISBN 978-1-0980-2677-6 (digital)

Christian Faith Publishing, Inc.
832 Park Avenue
Meadville, PA 16335
www.christianfaithpublishing.com

This is a work of fiction. Names, characters, places, events, and incidents are the result of the author's imagination. Any resemblance to actual persons living or dead or actual events is purely coincidental.

Printed in the United States of America

CHAPTER 1

It was June of 1884. Sixteen-year-old Ed loved life on the Kansas farm where he lived with his parents, John and Hilda Krehbiel, along with his three younger siblings, Willard (fifteen), Bertha (twelve), and Emma (nine). The quarter-section farm was purchased from the railroad just ten years ago, after they left Russia to make Kansas their new home. Leaving Russia guaranteed them they could worship God the way they pleased, and for Ed, it freed him of the certain threat that soon he would have to serve in the Russian military. Ed couldn't thank his parents, along with many other Mennonite families, enough for making that most difficult decision to leave Russia.

It seemed like there was always something for Ed to do on their farm. He was old enough now that most of the time, he would find something to do without being told.

Today at dinnertime, his mama asked him if he would hoe weeds in the garden. He was planning on helping his younger brother, Willard, or Bill, as everybody called him, fix the pigpen. One of their two sows was about to farrow, and the way the fence was, it would never keep in a litter of pigs. Bill insisted he could get the pigpen fixed himself, and

Hilda said she just had to finish the dress she was sewing for Bertha.

"That girl is growing so fast these days," she said, as she gave Ed one more pleading look to weed the garden.

"Okay, Mama, I'll weed the garden if Papa thinks Bill can get the pigpen fixed before that one sow farrows. But if I weed the garden, you must promise to make some mach kuchen just as soon as you finish that dress for Bertha."

"You drive a hard bargain, son," she said, then looked at her handsome husband, John, who was admiring his son because mach kuchen was one of his favorite things to eat also.

"Son, you better get to work on that garden right now. When I looked at it this morning, it was quite weedy, and I can almost taste some of that delicious mach kuchen already."

"Yes, Papa, I can almost taste it too," Ed replied as he grabbed his hat off the hook on the wall and went out the door, heading for the garden.

Almost three hours later, Ed had long since shed his shirt in the warm June sunshine and was wishing he could get rid of some more clothes; but if Mama saw him without a shirt, she would scold him because she thought it was inappropriate for men to work without a shirt even if they were working at home. Papa was usually a little more lenient in things like this, but in this case, he would take his wife's side about working without a shirt.

Ed looked up at the sun and figured it was getting close to milking time. Just then, he heard his papa call, "Ed, it is almost milking time. Are you about finished with the garden? You need to go get Bessy and Erma home so we can milk them?" Bessy and Erma were their two Jersey milk cows.

"Yes, Papa. I'll be finished in just a minute or two." Ed yelled back to his papa. Ed hurried hoeing the last few feet of the garden and hung the hoe up in the tool shed by the garden with the other garden tools. He grabbed his shirt off the post where he had hung it earlier and trotted over to the horse corral to get his almost–best friend Copper.

Copper was a sorrel gelding that John had traded for from one of the neighbors, Joe Flickner. Joe had hurt his back several years ago digging a well, and John offered to plow his field for him. He was more than happy to help Joe out for nothing because that was just what neighbors did, but then Joe insisted that John take the two-year-old gelding because he looked more like a riding horse than a workhorse. Joe said he had no use for a riding horse.

When John came home with the young gelding, Ed took one look at him and said, "Papa, you got me a riding horse. Just what I always wanted!"

"Well, son, do you think you can take care of him?"

"Oh, yes. I can take care of him. You don't have to worry about that, Papa! I know already what I will call him. He looks just like the color of copper. I'm going to call him Copper!"

"That's a fine name, son. Looks like you got a fine horse too."

"Thanks, Papa! Thank you so much! I love you, Papa!"

"I love you too, son. Now go take Copper and put him in the corral with the team of workhorses." From that day forward, whenever Ed had any spare time, he was working with Copper, training him to do what Ed wanted him to do.

As Ed was trotting to the horse corral, he whistled for Copper to come to him. Ed opened the corral gate, and Copper stepped outside the gate and waited for Ed. After Ed closed the gate, he turned toward Copper and took a couple of steps toward the gelding, grabbed a handful of mane, and easily swung onto Copper's back in one smooth motion. In the few years that Ed had Copper, he had trained him to ride without a saddle or even a bridle. To make Copper go forward, Ed would click his tongue and nudge Copper's sides slightly with his heels. The harder he nudged his heels, the faster Copper would go. To turn left, he simply used pressure with his right leg to get Copper to turn left; and to go right, it was his left leg that he used. To stop, he used the vocal command of "whoa." The louder the "whoa," the shorter Copper stopped. When Ed was on Copper, it was like the young man and horse were one.

That day, Ed pointed Copper toward the southwest corner of the pasture and set him at an easy gallop. He knew that would be where Bessy and Erma would be grazing. In the low spot of that area of the pasture, there were some cottonwood trees for shade; and beyond the cottonwood trees, there was a sand plum thicket that the cows loved to lie down by in the lush green grass.

Ed guided Copper through the cottonwood trees and then saw Bessy and Erma right where he figured they would be. He said, "All right, girls. It is that time again, and we need the milk so, let's get you home."

Ed guided Copper behind the cows as they slowly got to their feet to start toward the barn. Just as Copper was turning away from the plum thicket, Ed glanced over the thicket to the other side. Then he saw it. "Whoa, Copper," Ed said. He strained his neck to get a better look at what was behind the plum thicket. He couldn't believe his eyes what he saw.

CHAPTER 2

"Back, Copper," Ed asked of his sorrel gelding. The horse backed up a few steps until Ed said, "Whoa," and Copper stopped. Ed hoped at this vantage point, a little closer to the plum thicket, he would be able to see what was behind it. He strained his neck to get a better look. There was something there all right, but just when he looked over the thicket, whatever it was moved a little closer to the thicket so Ed couldn't see. It must have been some kind of an animal, but then he thought, *That sure did not look like any kind of animal I had ever seen before. In fact, it looked more like a human.* But it did not look like a human either. What was it?

Ed was just getting ready to have Copper walk around to the other side of the thicket so he could get a good look at what was behind there, then decided he had better follow Bessy and Erma home and get them milked. He clicked his tongue, nudged Copper with both heels, and set him at a slow trot to catch up with the two cows.

When Copper was a short distance behind the cows, Ed slowed him down to match the slow pace of the cows. His mind drifted back to the plum thicket, and he pondered some more about what it was he saw behind it. He decided to go back to the thicket after he finished milking Bessy and Erma, so he was in kind of a hurry; but he sure did not want to make the cows run on the way home because then, they would not give their milk.

Ed formed his plan for going back in the pasture after milking to find out what was behind the plum thicket. Going out into the pasture after the cows were milked was kind of unusual because the cows were kept in the barn for the night or in the small corral by the barn where they were given some hay and a little corn to munch on overnight.

As Copper slowly walked behind the cows, Ed could not get his mind off what he saw behind the plum thicket. The more he thought about it, the more confused he was by what he saw. It almost had to be a human, but if it was, why did it look like that? He just had to find out. If he hurried with the milking and the chores, afterwards, there would be plenty of daylight left for him to go back to look around.

When they arrived at the barn, Bessy and Erma needed no herding to go into the barn. Bessy went into the stanchion on the right, and Erma went on the left just like always. Ed closed the barn door from the back of Copper then trotted him over to the horse corral, slid off, opened the gate, and Copper trotted in. Ed closed the corral gate and hurried to the house to get the milk pails and back to the barn where he found Bessy and Erma patiently waiting for him to milk them.

Ed found the milk stool in the corner of the barn, picked it up, and took it over to Bessy. He sat down on the one-legged milk stool and started milking. He always milked Bessy first, and then Erma. He had no particular reason for doing it that way, but Bessy usually gave just a little more milk than Erma. She usually filled the milk pail about three fourths full, and Erma would fill the other pail just over half full. This evening was no exception.

When Ed had both cows milked, he took the milk to the house, set the milk pails on the bench in the kitchen, and said, "Mama, here is the milk. As soon as I finish up with the chores, I'm going back out to that sand plum thicket to pick some so you can make sand plum cobbler. You know how much Bill and I love your sand plum cobbler."

"Good lands, son. Earlier today, you ordered mach kuchen. Now you want cobbler. You think all I have to do is cook for you and your brother and sisters? Are you sure those sand plums are ripe already?"

"Yes, Mama. I think there are just enough to make one good size cobbler. I'll need a small bucket or something to put them in."

"Okay, son. Go finish your chores and I'll find something for you to put those sand plums in."

"Thanks, Mama. I'll be right back." Ed ran back down to the barn, climbed up to the hayloft, and threw two large pitch forks full of hay down for the two cows then slid down the ladder that went up to the hayloft. He had done that so often that he had the ladder slicked up and didn't even have to worry about splinters anymore. When he was back down on the main floor of the barn, he went to the corn bin, scooped up a small bucket of corn, and spread it out in the trough that was right beside the hay manger.

The cows usually ate the corn first then munched on the hay for a while.

He checked on the two hogs just to make sure Bill had fed them and to see if the one was ready to farrow tonight. Ed found them contentedly eating, and he was pretty sure that the one would not farrow yet tonight. As he walked to the house to get the bucket for the sand plums, he noticed that Bill had all the chickens penned up in the chicken coop. He was proud his younger brother was finally becoming more dependable with getting his chores done.

Finally, he was ready to head back out to that sand plum thicket to see what was back there. "Mama, I'll be back for supper with this bucket full of sand plums."

"Don't be long, Ed. Supper will be ready in less than an hour."

"Don't worry, Mama I'll be back in time with some nice, ripe sand plums," Ed said as he grabbed the small bucket his mama had set out for him.

As soon as he got out of the house, Ed whistled for Copper. He walked up to the gate, opened it, and Copper walked through. Ed closed the gate, turned, and swung onto Copper's back. He clicked his tongue, nudged Copper's sides with his heels, and had him headed for the plum thicket at a good gallop.

As he neared the thicket, he gradually slowed Copper down so as not to scare off anything or anybody that might be hiding behind the thicket. When he was right beside the thicket, he stopped Copper and slid off. He walked slowly toward the area where he had seen that "thing." It was no longer there. He knelt down to look under the bushes, crawled on his hands and knees the length of the thicket twice to make sure he was not missing anything. Just when he was ready to stand up and give up his search, he noticed some sand plum seeds in the dirt. So he was right. It was a human that was hiding here and eating the sand plums! Most animals would have eaten the seeds also.

Now he had another dilemma. Whoever it was that had been here had eaten most of the ripe sand plums. What was he going to tell Mama, who was expecting a bucket full of nice, ripe sand plums to make some cobbler? He found a few almost ripe ones that barely covered the bottom of the bucket. He would have to be creative and think of something to tell Mama.

CHAPTER 3

Ed kept Copper at a walk almost all the way back to the horse corral. He just did not know what to tell his mama about the lack of sand plums. He thought about telling her that Copper was spooked at something and he dropped the bucket and spilled them all, but he knew Mama would ask why he didn't stop and pick them up. Another thought was, *The sand plums were so ripe and delicious I just couldn't stop eating them.*

No, that would never work. Mama would really scold him for doing that. "I better just tell the truth," Ed finally decided as he arrived at the horse corral gate.

He let Copper into the corral then went up the hayloft to throw down some hay for Copper and the team of workhorses that Copper shared the corral with. While Copper was munching on some hay, Ed got the horse brush and brushed him down. When he was finished with that, he decided it was time to take the bucket with just a handful of plums in it to the house and try to explain to his mama why there were so few sand plums.

When he walked into the house, his mama said, "There you are, Ed. Just in time for supper. Set that bucket of sand plums on the work counter, and wash your hands and come sit down. Your brother and sisters act like they are about to starve. I'll get to those plums after supper."

Ed did as he was told and took his place at the table next to his papa who was at the end.

His papa looked at Ed and said, "Ed, the last one to the table always says grace."

"Yes, Papa," Ed said as he cleared his throat and bowed his head. "Dear Lord, we thank thee for this day. We thank thee for being with us and protecting us from all harm. Forgive us if we failed to do thy will. Bless this food to our nourishment. We ask these things in thy holy name. Amen."

Ed picked up the platter of Mama's fried chicken, took his favorite piece, a thigh, and passed the platter to Bill, then picked up the bowl of mashed potatoes and placed a couple of spoonful in his plate and passed the bowl on to Bill. Next came the gravy. Ed loved his mama's gravy, so he poured plenty on his mashed potatoes and passed the gravy bowl to Bill. Ed took a bite of his potatoes and gravy, swallowed hardly without chewing at all, then said, "Mama, there weren't enough sand plums to make even a very small cobbler."

"There weren't? What happened to them?" his mother asked.

"I think somebody ate all the ripe ones before I got back to pick them."

"What do you mean somebody ate them?" his mother asked.

"Well, when I was getting the cows home, I saw something behind the sand plum thicket. It must have been a person because when I got back out there, all I found was a pile of seeds," Ed explained.

"John, what is getting into people these days? Those sand plums are on our land. What makes other people think they can come and eat our sand plums?"

"Hilda, they are just sand plums. You don't need to get all worked up about it. My goodness, maybe somebody was very hungry and decided to stop and eat some. We don't have a sign out there telling people to stay away from our sand plums."

"I guess you're right, but it just surprises me what people do these days!"

"Mama, tomorrow, when I go get Bessy and Irma home for milking, I'll go a little early and see if I can catch whoever is eating our sand plums."

"Okay, son, but you be careful."

"I will, Mama. But I really don't think it's a bad man that is going to hurt me if I tell him he can't eat our sand plums."

"You be careful just the same," his mother warned.

The next day, after the morning chores were done, Ed helped his papa sharpen the scythes that they would soon be using to harvest the crop of Turkey Red winter wheat. It looked like they would have a pretty good crop this year, if only they could get it before something happened to it. This time of year, it was not uncommon for some pretty strong storms to roll across Kansas. What the farmers would wait for all winter and spring, Mother Nature could wipe out in just a few minutes with a bad hailstorm. It seemed like so much depended on the wheat crop every year.

When they had all their scythes sharpened and ready for harvest, Ed said, "Papa, I'm going to see if I can find out who is getting the sand plums."

"Well, son, it is a little early yet to bring the cows home for milking, but your mama is sure concerned about that sand plum thief."

"Yes, she is, Papa. I would just like to have some good warm cobbler for supper."

"There you go, son. I'm with you about the cobbler."

Ed wiped off his oily hands on a rag and headed toward the horse corral for Copper. When he was about at the corral, he whistled for Copper, and he came trotting to the gate. Ed opened the gate, and Copper walked out and waited for Ed to close the gate and swing unto his back. Ed pointed Copper toward the southwest corner of the pasture, and they were off at a good gallop.

Ed had decided he would leave Copper in the grove of cottonwood trees, then walk up to the plum thicket on foot. He was so certain that today, he would find whoever it was eating the sand plums, and he did not want to scare off him or her. He slowed Copper to a walk as they neared the tall cottonwood trees. In the middle of the grove of trees, he stopped Copper, slid to the ground, and started walking as quietly as he could to the sand plum thicket.

If there was someone there, they were on the far side again because there was nothing on the near side where he could see. Ed slowly walked to the edge of the thicket where he could see on the other side. There it was, only about fif-

16

teen feet away. It had the shape of a person. A young girl in fact, but she did not look like any of the Mennonite girls Ed had ever seen before. All the Mennonite girls he knew had light brown or blond hair, and this girl's hair was long and coal black. She had not yet noticed Ed looking at her, so he cleared his throat slightly to get her attention. It startled her, and she jumped to her feet and started to run away but then stopped and turned to look at Ed.

When Ed saw her eyes, it almost startled him. Every girl, in fact everybody he knew, had blue or hazel eyes, and a few people had green eyes. But this girl had brown eyes. He had never seen brown eyes before. He blinked his own eyes just to make sure he was not seeing things then he noticed something else about this girl. To go along with the black hair and brown eyes, her skin was dark, like she had a very deep suntan, and she had about the prettiest face he had ever seen. He knew a few very pretty Mennonite girls, but they had nothing over this girl.

Ed took a step or two nearer to the girl. He wanted to touch her to make sure she was real. As he reached out his hand to touch her arm, she pulled back slightly, but then gave Ed a smile that would have melted the heart of any sixteen-year-old American boy. Then she turned and ran off.

Ed called out to her, "Wait! Wait! Please don't go! I won't hurt you. You can eat all the sand plums you like!"

It was no use. When the girl reached the end of the plum thicket, she turned slightly to her right to put the thicket between her and Ed, and was soon out of sight.

CHAPTER 4

Ed just stood there for a moment, not believing what had just happened. How was he going to tell his parents, especially his mama, that the sand plump thief was about the prettiest girl he had ever seen? To say the least, a girl like that was the last thing he had expected to be the plum thief.

Ed shook his head to clear his mind of what he had just seen, and then turned to walk back to the cottonwood grove where Copper was patiently waiting just where Ed had left him. He grabbed a handful of mane, swung onto Copper's back, and headed him toward the barn. Before riding too far, he remembered that in all the excitement, he forgot about the cows. He started to turn Copper around to get the cows, when he spotted them walking by themselves toward the barn. He nudged Copper with his heels into a gallop to catch up with them but slowed Copper down in time not to run the cows.

Again, he had that troubled thought. *What am I going to tell Mama?* Today, he knew who the thief was; but if he would tell her it was a very pretty girl with long black hair, brown eyes, and the skin almost the color of Copper, his mama would probably scold him for lying to her. Maybe it wouldn't be so wrong to tell one little fib. What else could he do?

When he got home with the cows, Ed hurriedly did the milking and feeding so he could get into the house and get the inevitable over with. The last thing he did before going in was to check on the sow that was about to farrow. He was pretty sure tonight would be the night, and that would give him an excuse to come back out right after supper to check on her, and hopefully avoid too many questions about the sand plum thief.

When Ed got inside with the milk and set it on the bench like always, he said, "Here's the milk, Mama. I have to go back out right after supper to keep an eye on that sow so she doesn't step on her little pigs. I'm sure she will farrow tonight."

"Okay, son. Just calm down and get washed up for supper. It is just about ready. If that sow hasn't started farrowing already, there is plenty of time to eat your supper and get back out there. Those things just take time."

Ed did as his mama told him and took his seat at the table. This evening, his father was the last one to the table, so he led in saying grace. Ed thought that was the way God really intended it to be because he felt Papa handled it so much better than anybody else.

When all the food had been passed around and everyone had started eating, Papa looked at Ed and said, "Well, son, what is the latest on the sand plum thief? Do you know today who it is?"

Ed felt his face turn pale. He was about to have to lie to his papa. "Yes, I do, Papa. I know who it is."

"Well, do you want to tell us, or are you going to keep us in suspense?" his papa asked.

Then Ed's youngest sister, Emma, piped up, "Please, Eddy, tell us already. I can't stand it any longer!"

Bertha looked at her younger sister and said, "Give him time, Emma. He has to think about how to tell us how ugly the evil man looked so you don't have nightmares about him tonight."

Emma looked up at her older sister and said, "I haven't had a nightmare for a long time."

"All right, all right, girls, that's enough," their mama said. She looked at Ed and said simply, "Son?"

Ed realized he couldn't put it off any longer. He had to lie to his parents. Not wanting to look either his papa or his mama in the eye, he looked down at his lap and said very quietly, "It was just a very small girl. I didn't know her. I think she was from the other Mennonites that live south of here. I told her those were our sand plums and not to come back because she was stealing."

"Those people! How they raise their children, just letting them steal like that!" Hilda huffed.

"Hilda!" John said. "You're getting all worked up over a few sand plums again. How many times do I have to tell you? They're just sand plums."

"I know, John. I shouldn't be like that, but I can't help it. Today, the child steals sand plums. What will it be tomorrow, a chicken, a sheep, or heaven forbid, somebody's milk cow?"

"Now, Hilda, that's enough!" John scolded his wife.

Ed just lost all his appetite. His papa was scolding his mama, and he was the one who should be getting a good scolding for lying like he did. "Mama, may I be excused? I'm not hungry anymore, and I have to go check on that sow."

"Son, what's got into you? You barely touched your meat loaf, and I made it just for you because you always say it's your favorite!"

"I know, Mama. The meat loaf is good, but I'm so worried about that sow and those little pigs she is about to have," Ed explained. "I can't eat anymore!"

"Okay, go on out to that sow. I'll save some of that meat loaf for you, and maybe when you come in, you'll be able to eat some more."

"Thanks, Mama!" Ed said as he got up from the table. He grabbed his hat from the hook on the wall and headed out the door to the pigpen.

Hilda looked at her husband and said, "John, do you know what got into that boy? He didn't even finish his meat loaf, and he usually has two or three helpings of it."

"Hilda, you need to settle down and not get so worked up over little things like this. Ed is a grown boy, and I'm sure he will eat when he gets hungry."

"I don't know how you can be so calm about everything, John. A thief, a growing boy who doesn't eat! What's next?"

"Mama, maybe Ed is in love and that is why he is not hungry," Bertha said.

With a very slight grin, John looked at his oldest daughter; and while shaking his head, he said, "Now is not the time, sweetheart."

"Okay, Papa. I'm sorry."

The thought of his oldest son being in love, like Bertha suggested, was something that had never crossed John's mind.

By the time Ed got back out to the pigpen, the first little pig was being born. Everything looked okay to Ed, so he found a log to sit down on and made himself comfortable. The pig somehow wiggled himself over to the side of his mama where supper was waiting for him and started to nurse. Ed wondered out loud, "How did that little pig just a few minutes old know there was something to eat over there?"

Then he remembered, just last Sunday in Sunday school at the New Land Mennonite Church where his papa took the family every Sunday, Mr. Waltner, his Sunday-school teacher said, "God has control over everything, and all we have to do is trust him and everything will be okay."

"I guess God has control over you too, little pig." Ed had to chuckle at himself for talking about God to a little pig.

Over the next forty-five minutes, six more pigs were born, and all wiggled over to their mama for their first supper. Just when the last one was being born, Ed's father came out to check on things. "How is it going, son? Is there any new life there already?"

"Yes, Papa. We have seven healthy little pigs!" Ed answered is father.

"Are they all eating good?" his father asked.

"Yes, Papa. They are all eating. These two are about to burst already. They were the first two born."

"Well, that will make some great bacon and ham in about a year!" His father said. Then he added, "Son, do you want me to take over for you, and you can go in and go to bed?"

"No, Papa. I'm okay. I want to stay out here."

"I'll go in and get a blanket and bring it out to you. It might be a little chilly toward morning. Do you want me to bring anything else?"

"Papa, that meat loaf Mama had for supper sure was good!"

"I'll bring you some of that too, son, and a tall glass of milk."

In a few minutes, Ed's father returned with the promised goods and gave them to Ed. "Here you go, son. You're all set for the night."

"Thank you so much, Papa. I love you, Papa."

"I love you too, son. Now you have a good night with those little pigs."

CHAPTER 5

Ed sat down on the log again and looked at the large plate of meat loaf and potatoes that his father had brought out to him. It did look better than it did at the supper table, but Ed still wasn't really hungry. He took a bite of the meat loaf anyway and then a bite of potatoes, and realized how hungry he really was. In no time at all, he had the plate cleaned out. "Thanks, Mama. That sure was good!" He said even though he knew his mama could not hear him in the house.

Ed glanced over at the mama sow with her seven new pigs and saw that everyone, including the mama, seemed to be very content. Ed was pretty sure they would all stay that way until morning. He grabbed the blanket his father had brought him and wrapped himself up in it, leaned against the log, closed his eyes, and tried to catch a little sleep. That did not work at all. As soon as he closed his eyes, he saw the pretty face of the girl by the sand plums. He remembered that he had to lie to his family about her and felt so bad again about that.

How did he ever get himself in such a dilemma that had no way out? If he was honest with himself, he knew he wanted to go to the sand plum thicket in the worst way, just to see that girl with the black hair and brown eyes again. Those thoughts kept Ed awake most of the night. About the time the eastern sky was turning a little gray, he was able to dose off for a few minutes.

Just as the sun was coming up, the squealing of one of the pigs woke him abruptly. Ed jumped to his feet and saw that while the mama sow was trying to stand up, she was stepping on one of the pig's tail. The pig didn't know how lucky he was that it was just his tail getting stepped on and not his whole body. Ed stepped over to the mama sow and gently nudged her over to get her back foot off the tail of the pig. She walked to the feed trough and started eating, and the freed pig scampered over to join his brothers and sisters who were all in a group, worried about being so far away from their mama.

Ed was wondering who was going to come and relieve him so he could go in and get some breakfast.

Just then, Bill appeared and asked, "How was your night, Ed? Did all the pigs survive until morning?"

"Yes, all the pigs are still alive. One had his tail stepped on, but he survived that, of course. He did a lot of squealing about it though and that woke me up from my short night's sleep. Are you here to relieve me, Bill, so I can get some breakfast?"

"Yes, Ed. That is the plan. I have not done any of the morning chores yet, so if you take care of that, I can be here until dinnertime, for sure."

"Okay, Bill. I'll be happy to do your chores for you. You won't have much to do until mama sow finishes eating and comes back to lie down so her pigs can nurse. When she does, just make sure she doesn't lay on any of the pigs."

"Okay. I'll watch them, Ed."

Ed was confident in his younger brother's ability to keep the mama sow from doing any harm to her pigs, so he left and started on the morning chores. First, he took care of the ones he usually did, like the milking of the cows, then feeding them and the horses.

Next, he let the chickens out of the coop and gathered the eggs. After that, he went over to the sheep barn, gave them some hay in the manger outside, and let them all out of the barn. When all that was done, he went to the house with the milk and the eggs.

"Well, good morning, son. How are the pigs this morning, and did you get any sleep last night?"

"Mama, the pigs are all okay, and no, I did not get much sleep. But I'll be okay."

"How many eggs would you like for breakfast, son, three or four, with a couple of slices of bacon?"

"Yes, Mama. Four will be fine and a couple slices of bacon."

"Oh, before your papa left this morning, he said since you were up all night with the pigs, you can take a nap if you want because the wheat is not quite ready to cut for a few days and there is nothing too pressing."

"Oh, that sounds good. I sure won't take a nap though. I have too many things to do for that. I need to take Copper for a ride. I haven't just gone for a ride for pleasure for a long time." He knew already where he would go, but he didn't say anything to his mama.

"Thanks a lot for breakfast, Mama! It sure was good. I may not be home for dinner, but don't worry about me, those four eggs and bacon will take me to suppertime."

"Are you sure, son? You're a growing boy and need to eat. Here, I just happen to have a ham sandwich in the ice-box." She went to get it, put it in a bag, and gave it to him.

"Thanks, Mama. I love you. Mama!"

"Love you too, son!"

Ed grabbed his hat off the hook and loped out the door to the horse corral. He whistled at Copper who came trotting to the gate and waited for Ed to open it so he could walk out. After Ed closed the gate, as was his habit, he grabbed a handful of mane, swung onto Copper's back, and pointed him to the sand plum thicket at an easy gallop.

As he rode, he wondered what was wrong with his mama. It just wasn't like her not to ask where he was going and why he was going there. He was sure glad she didn't ask because he did not want to talk about the sand plum thief with her. He was sure the girl would be there early today. He didn't know why; he just had a feeling she would be there.

As he approached the cottonwood grove, he slowed Copper down to a walk. When he was about the middle of the grove, he stopped Copper and slid off. He didn't know what to do with the bag containing the sandwich, so he took it with him. When he came out of the cottonwood grove, he stopped for a moment to look if he could see the girl any place. There she was toward the east end of the thicket with her back toward him.

Ed saw her coal-black hair hanging almost to her waist. Ed couldn't help but just stare at her for a moment. Then he felt guilty, took a few more steps toward her, and cleared his throat to get her attention.

She immediately turned around and for a brief moment, just looked at him. Then she greeted him with that same heart-melting smile that she said goodbye to him with yesterday. Ed slowly took a step closer to her and reached out his hand to touch her. She did not turn and run like yesterday but instead, slowly extended her hand so Ed could take it and hold it. For a moment, neither of them moved, and Ed just looked into those big brown eyes of hers. He had never seen eyes that beautiful before.

All the Mennonite girls Ed knew all wore long cotton dresses. This girl was wearing something that looked like leather but seemed to be very soft, and it only came down to about her knees. *I'll take that over a long cotton dress any day*, Ed thought.

In a moment, he asked in his native German dialect. "What is your name?"

With disappointment in her eyes, she said in a different German dialect, "I don't understand."

Ed could not believe his ears. She could speak the German dialect of the other Mennonites that lived in a community just a few miles south of where they were. Ed could not speak that German, but he knew what it was when he heard it spoken. He was not going to give up that easily in trying to communicate with this beautiful girl. He asked in broken English, "Do you speak English?"

The girl's eyes lit up, and she said, "Yes, yes, I speak English!" With excitement in her voice, she asked in English, "What is your name?"

Again, in broken English, Ed said, "My name is Ed. What is your name?"

The girl said, "My name is Sasha. It means 'running water' in my native tongue."

CHAPTER 6

Ed couldn't remember when he ever had to put that much effort into learning a girl's name. He had so many things he wanted to ask Sasha, but he did not know where to start. First, his limited ability with the English language was going to be a challenge, and how in the world did Sasha know English so well? Where did she come from? How did she know the German that some Mennonites spoke, and how was he going to learn all that with his limited English?

Sasha could see all the questions in his eyes. She squeezed his hand to reassure him and said, "Come, follow me. I know a nice place where we can talk."

Ed started to follow and then remembered Copper. He couldn't leave him in the middle of the grove that long. Ed had a feeling this could take some time getting to know Sasha. He said, "Wait a minute." He whistled at Copper, and the horse came trotting.

"Very beautiful horse," Sasha said. She reached out to scratch Copper's neck. "What is his name?"

"Copper, and he is very smart," Ed said.

Sasha continued to scratch Copper's neck for a moment, then said, "He has lots of grass to eat here. Will he stay here?"

Ed nodded, "Yes, he'll stay where I tell him to."

"Okay," Sasha said. "Come, follow me, and we can sit and talk." She took Ed's hand and started walking toward the south.

Ed could not believe how Sasha asserted herself and the confidence she displayed. He knew no Mennonite girl would have been brave enough to scratch the neck of a strange horse, or for that matter, to tell a boy she just met to follow her.

After they crossed the southern border of Ed's father's land, they walked a short way farther and came to a small stream with crystal-clear water running in it. Ed did not even know the stream was here. He had never been this far off their land.

Sasha led the way to two large rocks next to the stream that were almost in the shape of chairs. She sat down on the rock next to the stream and gestured for Ed to take a seat on the other rock.

Ed sat down and looked around at their surroundings for a moment and thought, *This has to be the place God created especially for young people to come to get to know each other.* He had not seen a more beautiful place. Along the stream, there were a few tall oak trees for shade, and they all had birds singing in them. Ed could even see a few fish in the stream. The stream had lush green grass on either side. Scattered through the grass were some red and purple prairie rose flowers.

After a little bit of looking over the place, he let his eyes fall on Sasha. He could not believe how incredibly beautiful she was.

She smiled at him and said, "This is a very pretty place."

"Yes, it is," replied Ed. "How did you know about it?"

Sasha raised her hand to point to the southeast. "I live just a few miles over there. I live with some Mennonites. They are my family."

"Wait, wait," Ed said. "Why do you live with Mennonites? You must be Indian."

Sasha smiled, "Okay, let me start from the beginning. First, we don't call ourselves Indian. My tribe was Kancha, and we lived that direction." She pointed to the southwest and continued, "We lived there for many years. Some years ago, the white man came, and my people started to get sick with diseases we never had before. We had no cure for these diseases. Many people died. It was a sad time. In a few years, what we called the Blue Coats started to come. They rode horses, and they killed many of our people in different villages for no reason. It seemed like the people that didn't die from disease were killed by the Blue Coats. One day, when I was about five years old, the Blue Coats came to my village. They were shooting everybody, even women and small children. Just before they killed my mother, she pulled me to the ground and lay on top of me. I stayed under her until all the shooting stopped, and then when I heard no more talking, I crawled out from under my mother. She saved my life! I was the only one in the village still alive."

Sasha paused for a moment and then started to cry uncontrollably. Ed had to wipe some tears from his own eyes. How could some people be so cruel to other people? He put his arms around Sasha and gently pulled her close to him. This same girl who just a short time ago showed so much confidence was now crying like a small child. Ed's heart was breaking for her. He wanted to hold her in his arms forever.

Shortly, Sasha was able to gain control of her crying, but Ed continued to hold her. In a moment, she gently pushed back from him and wiped her face with her hands.

"I'm sorry for crying. You are so kind to hold me like that. Thank you. I have not been held like that for a long time. It felt so good."

"I am so sorry all your people were killed by Blue Coats. What happened to you after that?" Ed asked.

Sasha continued with her story. "Remember, I was only five and I was all by myself. I wondered around our village for two days, maybe three. I'm not sure. Before they left, the Blue Coats took all our food and water with them. There was nothing for me to eat or drink. I was so hungry and thirsty. I think it was the third day just before sundown that some men came. At first, I hid from them, but then I saw they did not look like the Blue Coats, so I let them find me. The one who found me picked me up and gave me some water to drink. It tasted so good. I wanted to drink some more, but he made me wait awhile then he gave me more.

"All these men had hair on their face. I had never seen that before. They were kind to me and took me to their homes. The women gave me some soup to eat. It was delicious. I think I ate three bowls full. Then they gave me a bath in warm water. Oh, that felt so good.

"I have been living with one couple ever since. They have no other children. Their names are Samuel and Maria Regier. They are good people, and they treat me well. They sent me to school with all the other children. At first, I did not like going to school. The teacher was mean to me, and she sometimes slapped my hands with a stick if I did something wrong or didn't understand something. The next year, we got a different teacher. She was very good to me. If I had trouble understanding something, she would even come to our house in the evening and help me. I will always be grateful to her."

"Sasha, how did you learn to speak English so well?" Ed asked.

"When I was very young and before the Blue Coats came to our village, my father was the chief. One day, a white man came who could speak a little of our tongue. He said my father should learn English so he could negotiate with the white man when they wanted to make a new treaty. That man came almost every day for many days to teach my father English. When the white man would leave, my father would practice with me what the white man taught him. At that age, I learned English just as fast as I learned my native language. Now where I live, most of the children speak English, so I talk with them in English, and I talk with the grownups in their language. I think it is German."

Ed nodded and said, "You must be very intelligent. You speak three different languages."

Sasha smiled and said, "Thank you. You are very kind. Can you tell me about yourself now? I have told you all about myself. Are you a Mennonite like Samuel and Maria Regier?"

Ed was going to explain to her that yes, he was Mennonite, but not like them, when he noticed that the sun was almost straight up. He asked, "Sasha, are you hungry? I have a sandwich we can share."

Ed reached behind him and got the sandwich he had kept out of sight all this time, unwrapped it, and showed it to Sasha.

"Oh, that looks so good. I have a bottle of cold milk in the stream." She stepped down from the rock and took a step toward the stream. She reached down in the water, retrieved a large bottle of milk, and held it up for Ed to see. "This should be very cold by now," she said.

Ed smiled and gestured for her to sit back down. He tore the sandwich in half and gave Sasha half of it. Then Ed said, "I always pray before I eat. Do you mind?"

"Samuel and Maria have taught me to pray also."

They both bowed their heads and Ed said a short prayer in his native German dialect. When he had finished, they both took a bite of their sandwich.

Sasha said, "This sandwich is delicious!" Then she took a drink of milk and handed the bottle to Ed.

When he was still drinking, Sasha asked, "What did you say to God when you prayed?"

Ed finished his drink and said, "First, I thanked God for letting me meet such a beautiful girl, and then I thanked him for the sandwich and milk.

Sasha smiled and said, "That was nice. I prayed the same thing. I thanked him for letting me meet a boy who is so handsome and treats me so nice, and for even sharing his sandwich with me." When they both finished their sandwiches, Sasha said, "Thank you, Ed. That was a very good sandwich. Now you must tell me about yourself."

Ed nodded, took another drink of the cold milk, passed the bottle back to Sasha, and said, "Thank you for the cold milk, Sasha. It was good with our sandwich."

She nodded and placed the nearly empty bottle on the rock beside her.

Ed took both of Sasha's hands in his and held them. In his broken English, he began to share about himself. "My family lived in Russia for many years. I was born in Russia. I have one brother and two sisters. Only my youngest sister was born in Kansas.

"We had a good life in Russia. Unfortunately, the leader changed, and the new leader said all boys must fight for their country. We are Mennonites, and Mennonites believe fighting is wrong. The new leader said we must fight, or we will be punished. My father and others made plans to leave Russia and come to Kansas. The trip from Russia to Kansas took several weeks. Many people died on the way. The first winter, we all lived in one big house the railroad built for us. It was crowded, drafty, and smelled bad. But we were very thankful for it. We have lived in Kansas about ten years now."

"Where do you live?" Sasha asked.

"I live on a farm about one mile north. My father bought 160 acres from the railroad. Our land comes up to that stake." He pointed to a yellow stake in the ground.

Sasha pulled her hands away from Ed to cover her face in embarrassment and asked, "Are those sand plums I have been eating on your land?"

Ed took her hands away from her face, held them again in his, and said, "Yes, they are our sand plums. But if you had not been eating them, I never would have met you. It's okay that you ate them."

Sasha smiled and said, "I'm glad I ate them, so I got to meet you too. They are very sweet and delicious!"

Ed laughed a little and said, "If you leave enough ripe ones, I'll take them home, and Mama will make sand plum cobbler. I'll bring you some to eat."

"I have never had sand plum cobbler, but it must be good. I promise to leave enough for your mama to make some," Sasha said.

Ed looked up at the sky and saw that the sun was at about mid-afternoon already. "I'm sorry, Sasha. I must go home. My parents will worry about me if I don't come home."

Sadness showed in Sasha's eyes, and she asked, "When will I see you again, Ed?"

"I don't know. I think on Monday, we'll start to harvest wheat. I have to help. Maybe in a week, I'll come back. I'll wait for you here."

Sadness deepened in Sasha's eyes as she said, "A week is a long time. I will think of you every day. But in a week, I'll be here waiting for you."

"I promise I'll come in one week." Ed said. Ed whistled at Copper, and he immediately came trotting to him.

Sasha said, "You have a very smart horse."

Suddenly, Ed realized that he was able to ride home, and this pretty girl had to walk. He asked, "Sasha, may I take you home?"

She looked at him with a big smile and said, "Will you please, cowboy?"

Ed laughed. He had only heard the word "cowboy" one other time in his life and wasn't sure what Sasha meant by it, but he grabbed a handful of Copper's mane and swung unto his back. Before he was barely set, Sasha grabbed his arm and swung on behind him. He couldn't believe how easily and gracefully she did it. There wasn't a white Mennonite girl in all of Kansas that could have done that.

"Do you want the milk bottle?" Ed asked.

"Yes, please," Sasha replied.

Ed guided Copper close to the rock, and Sasha swooped down and picked the bottle gingerly off the rock.

"Show me where you live, Sasha," Ed said.

She pointed to the southeast and said, "About two miles that way, but you will have to let me off before we reach the farm of Samuel and Maria. If they see me with a white boy like you, they will be upset."

"I understand," replied Ed. He set Copper at a slow, easy gallop. Ed was sure Sasha could have stayed on Copper without holding on at all, but she had her arms wrapped tightly around his waist. He did not mind that at all.

Just before they topped a small hill, Sasha said, "I think you should let me off here. The farm is just over the hill."

Ed brought Copper to a stop. Sasha said, "This has been a great day for me. I will see you by the stream in one week."

Ed nodded and said, "One week."

Sasha took his arm and slid down to the ground.

Just before she let go of his arm, he took her hand in his, bent down, kissed the back of her hand, and said, "You are the most beautiful girl I know!"

Sasha smiled then said, "Goodbye, Ed."

Ed watched Sasha until she disappeared over the hill. He turned Copper around, clicked his tongue, and set him at a good gallop headed toward home. He knew this would be the longest week of his life.

CHAPTER 7

Ed had ridden just a short way when less than an hour of sleep the previous night hit him all at once. He could hardly keep his eyes open. He thought he better slow Copper down in case he fell asleep and fell off. He could get hurt at the speed they were going. He knew Copper would stop if he did fall off, but still, he could get hurt. He slowed Copper down to a slow gallop but that seemed like a rocking chair trying to rock him to sleep.

He let his mind go back to the pretty girl he was with just a few minutes earlier. All at once, the thought struck him: what would his parents say about him spending time with a beautiful Indian girl? Beautiful or not, they would not accept that at all! Mennonites were supposed to associate only with their own people. Sasha was far from one of them. But wait, didn't she pray before they ate, just like Ed? That meant she believed in God just as Ed did. Weren't they both children of God?

But then, Ed could hear his mama already if he told her. "Ed, she is different than we are! She is an Indian! Do you really want to marry an Indian? They are completely different than we are! They believe differently than we do!

Ed, you have to sit down and ask yourself, do you really want to do this?"

The thought of going home and telling his parents what he was doing today, and their reaction to it, almost made him sick to his stomach. Sasha was the sweetest girl he had ever met; and just because her skin, hair, and eyes were a different color than they were used to, they would not accept her.

Ed slowed Copper down to a walk so he could think better. He almost felt like not going home, but where would he go? What would he do? That would not be right. He had to go home and tell them who he was with today.

When he got to their farm, it looked like most of the evening chores were done already. The cows were behind the barn, eating hay; the sheep had been penned up; and the chickens were all in their coop. He rode Copper to the corral gate, slid down to the ground, opened the gate, and let Copper walk in. He would have to throw some hay down for the horses, and he wanted to brush down Copper.

Bill showed up just when he was starting to brush Copper and asked, "Where in the world have you been all day, Ed? You surely have not been with the sand plum thief all day, have you?"

Ed thought Bill didn't realize how close to correct he was, but now when he thought about it, he did not think of Sasha as the sand plum thief anymore. He thought of her as the most beautiful girl he knew.

"I'll tell you all about it at supper," Ed said. He wished he hadn't said that because there was just no way he could tell his family about Sasha. "Bill, do you know what Mama made for supper?" Ed asked.

"I'm not sure, but when I took the milk and eggs in, it smelled like pork chops."

"That sounds good," Ed said without too much enthusiasm. With what he had to tell his parents, he was not sure he would be able to eat anything for supper.

Ed finished brushing Copper, put the brush away, and followed his younger brother into the house.

"Well, there you are, Ed. We were wondering if you would show up for supper," his papa said.

"Where have you been all day?" Mama asked. "Get washed up. Supper is ready."

Bill beat Ed to the wash sink so that meant he would also beat him to the table, and Ed would have to say grace. Ed wondered what he would say. He sure could not lie to God. When Bill finished at the sink, Ed went to wash, then took his place at the table.

Ed's papa looked at him and said, "Ed."

Ed cleared his throat and began. "Lord, it has surely been a blessed day today. I thank thee for thy goodness shone to me today. I pray for more days like this, if it be thy will. We thank thee for this food and ask you to bless the hands that prepared it. In thy name, we pray. Amen."

After the food had all been passed around, Papa said, "Ed, from the sound of your prayer, you must have had a good day today. Do you want to tell us about it?"

"Yes, Papa. I have a lot to tell you." He began, "First, I lied to you yesterday when I told you the sand plum thief was a little girl." Ed could feel all the eyes of his family turn to him when he said he had lied. "The truth is she is about my age. Her name is Sasha."

"Did you say Sasha?" his mama interrupted. "What kind of name is Sasha? Does she have a last name?"

Ed did not know what to say. Sasha did not really have a last name. All at once, he blurted out, "I think it is Regier. Yes, now I remember she said Regier."

"Oh, one of those other Mennonites! They don't even know how to name their own children! Why couldn't they name her something like Mary or Martha, or Anna, but Sasha? What a shame for a child to be called Sasha!"

"Now, Hilda, there you go getting yourself all worked up again! That is just wrong for you to do that!" Papa reminded her.

"Mama, I think you would like Sasha if you knew her. She is a very pretty girl," Ed replied. Ed was afraid he might have said too much. What would he say if Mama asked what color of hair and eyes Sasha had? He would be in real trouble then. He added, "Mama, Papa, as soon as we finish the wheat harvest, I am going to start courting Sasha. Maybe one day, she will marry me."

Mama got to her feet, and while shaking her pointing finger at Ed, she said, "Edward, you cannot do that! It is absolutely wrong to marry that girl!"

Then Papa added, "Son, haven't we always taught you that a marriage works best if we marry someone from our own people?"

Feeling very discouraged, Ed replied, "Yes, Papa, you have. But I can't see how Sasha and I are not the same. We are Mennonite and she is Mennonite. I believe in God and Sasha believes in God. That makes us both children of God." He looked at is mother and asked, "Am I not right, Mama?"

"Ed, it would be so much better if you married a girl like Anna Schrag. She is a very pretty girl, and she is about your age," Mama said.

"I know, Mama, but Robert Gering told me last Sunday at church he wanted to start courting Anna."

"Well, there are other girls just as pretty," his mother said.

Feeling defeated, Ed asked, "Mama, may I go to bed? I hardly had any sleep at all last night."

"Sure, son, but you hardly touched your supper," Mama answered with a concerned look on her face.

"I know, Mama. The pork chops are very good, but I'm so tired."

Just as Ed was heading to his room, his father said, "Son, that other sow looks like she will farrow tonight. Do you want to look after her or should I?"

"I'll do it, Papa. You know that is my job." Ed grabbed his hat off the hook on the wall, walked out the door, and glumly headed for the pigpen.

CHAPTER 8

When Ed got to the pigpen, he couldn't believe his eyes. There were nine baby pigs nursing at their mama.

"Well, it doesn't look like you need me very much. But I think I'll stay anyway. You probably won't lecture me about my girlfriend as much as Mama and Papa did. I wonder if the blanket is still out here that I had the other night. Right there. It is all folded up, just waiting for me. I'm surprised you didn't help yourself to it." Then he had to laugh at himself for talking to the pigs. He got the blanket, unfolded it, shook it good to get all the critters out, and wrapped himself up in it.

Just then, his father appeared. "Ed, is there someone else out here with you?" he asked. "I thought I heard you talking to someone when I was walking down here."

"No, Papa," Ed replied. "I was just talking to this old sow and her litter of pigs. Look, she has nine of them."

"Well, I'll be!" his father exclaimed. "And they're all okay?"

"Yes, Papa. They are all fine," Ed said.

"This sow has had three or four litters already, so she has more experience at it. She probably won't give you any problems at all," Papa said with a smile.

"No, I don't think so," Ed agreed.

Papa turned to head back to the house, then stopped, and with concern in his voice said, "Son, before I left the house, your mama said I should tell you that she felt bad the way she scolded you at supper. But you have to understand that she loves all you kids so much, and she really does want the best for all of you."

"I know, Papa. I love you and Mama very much too, and I'm so thankful I have a mama and papa like you."

Then his father kind of winked at Ed and said, "She hopes this will make up for the scolding." He handed Ed something wrapped up in paper.

Ed looked at it and was about to ask, "What is it?" when his papa smiled and said, "It's the mach kuchen she promised us a couple of days ago."

Ed ripped the paper off and took a big bite. "This is really good," he said.

His father handed him a bottle of milk. "This is to wash it down with. I'll see you in the morning, son."

The bottle of milk immediately reminded him of Sasha. It was good, but not as cold as the bottle she had. "I wonder if she likes mach kuchen."

Ed wondered if she had told Samuel and Maria that she spent most of the day with a white boy, and if she got a scolding like he did. In a moment, the thought struck him. *Why were they not trying to take away her Indian heritage?* He was glad they were not, but it was a little strange. He had heard that if the whites were not killing the Indians, they were trying to make them white. He felt that was wrong. That was the last thought he had as he fell into a deep sleep.

The sun was well up in the sky when Ed awoke the next morning. He was pleased to see the mama sow at the trough eating, and all the pigs were in one bunch waiting for their mama to lie down so they could have their breakfast too.

Ed couldn't believe he hadn't even finished the mach kuchen his papa brought him last night. He was glad he was still awake enough to place it on the piece of paper that his mama had wrapped it in and not on the ground. He picked it up, surveying it to see if any wild critters had nibbled on it during the night. When it appeared untouched by any critters, he took a little bite of it. He quickly determined it was still just as good as it was last night, and it was all gone in a couple more bites. The wild critters probably wouldn't have liked it any way, he decided with a smile.

In a few minutes, his father and younger brother Bill showed up. Bill said, "Well, you sleepy head, you finally woke up. We were here earlier, and you were still sound asleep. I wanted to kick you or something to wake you up, but Papa told me to let you sleep. Did you have a good night?"

"Yes, I did, Bill, and thanks for not waking me up. I was dog tired last night," Ed replied gratefully.

"Boys, your mama said breakfast was ready, so we better go in and eat," Papa said.

At the breakfast table, after all the eggs, bacon, and biscuits had been passed around, Papa said, "Listen, everyone, I have been checking the wheat, and I am sure it will be ready on Monday. We three men will be doing the cutting. When we cut it, we will be placing it in small bundles, and then Bertha and Emma will pick up the bundles and make shocks out of them. That is simply standing the wheat up so all the heads are up and off the ground, and can dry out."

Emma, the youngest, said, "Papa, I've never done that before. What if I don't know how to do it?"

Bertha promptly reassured Emma, "Don't worry, it is not that hard. I did it last year, and it is pretty easy. I'll show you some tricks to make it stand up and not fall over."

"Thank you, Bertha," their father said with a smile. "You keep an eye on your little sister."

Feeling proud that Papa was placing that kind of responsibility on her, Bertha sat up a little straighter and said, "I will, Papa."

Seeing he had everyone's attention, Papa began, "Here is what I have planned. We will start on the northeast forty. That is all wheat. The southeast forty has twenty acres of wheat and twenty acres of oats. We will do the wheat first then just move right into the oats. We have ten acres of barley over in the northwest corner. That will be the last field we will do. Does everybody understand what we will be doing all next week?" There were no comments, just heads bobbing up and down in agreement.

Mama quickly spoke up, "Well, John, you didn't say you have anything for me to do. I think I'll just sit on the porch, drink tea, and watch all of you work."

Papa was quick to ask, "Kids, listen to your mama. She thinks she can just sit, drink tea, and watch us work. Do you all agree with her?"

There was a loud unison, "No, Mama. You have to feed us three times a day, bring lunch out in the afternoon, and bring water or lemonade when we get thirsty."

"Okay, I will be so happy to do all that for my family because they are all so good and I love them dearly," Mama said with a smile. Then she looked at her oldest son and said, "Ed, I'm so sorry for the way I talked to you last night. Can you ever forgive me?"

"Sure, Mama. I forgive you."

His mother put her arm on Ed's shoulder and said, "Ed, I'm sure Sasha is a very lovely young lady, and if that is the girl you want to spend the rest of your life with, then you have my blessing. But I want you to pray about it and ask God if she is the one he has chosen for you. Maybe it would be a good idea to talk to Rev. Schrag about it also and see what he says." Then with a thoughtful look on her face, she added, "Sasha isn't such a bad name. After you say it a few times, it is actually kind of a pretty name. It is different though."

"Thank you, Mama. I love you, Mama," Ed said with a sigh of relief.

On Sunday in church, Rev. Schrag's sermon was from 2 Corinthians 6:14, where Paul was telling the Christians not to be unequally yoked with non-Christians. Ed could feel his face start to get red, and then he thought, *He is not talking to me because Sasha definitely believes in God.*

Rev. Schrag went on to say, "And brothers and sisters, we can also say that being unequally yoked to someone who is different than us culturally, or maybe they have different interests than we do, or different family values than what we do is also not God's will."

Ed was not in agreement with Reverend Schrag. He thought, *You are drawing a pretty thin line to follow now. We all have different interests, don't we?* Ed planned to talk to Rev., Schrag after church but maybe today would not be the best day for that.

After the service was over, Rev. Schrag was at the west door of the church, shaking hands with as many people as he could. Ed was hoping somehow, he could take a detour around the reverend and not have to shake hands with him, but there was just no way he could get around it. When his turn came to shake the reverend's hand, he made sure he got a good hold of his hand, gripped it tight, and said, "Very good message, Rev. Schrag, and I learned something too."

"Well, thank you, young man. I appreciate you saying that, and thanks for being here today."

He knew the reverend didn't remember his name. That is why he called him young man, but that was okay.

When they got home from church, Mama put the chicken noodle soup on the stove to heat it up. That was the usual Sunday after-church dinner. Papa got his Bible down from the mantle and had it ready to read from as soon as Mama had the soup on the table. It was the same ritual that took place every Sunday. Mama would heat up the soup, and Papa would read from the Bible, sometimes until the soup was cold again, and nobody could eat until Papa was finished reading.

There were a few things like this that Ed could not figure out about his parents, but for the most part, he thought his parents were great and was thankful he had good parents.

When they had all finished eating, Ed asked to be excused and said he was going to take a nap until it was time to do the evening chores.

CHAPTER 9

On Monday, about midmorning, after the dew had dried from the wheat, the family started the harvest. Both boys had run the scythes several years already, but like many things, it took a while until they found the rhythm and efficiency they had at the end of last wheat harvest.

Bertha was patiently teaching her younger sister how to place the bundles of wheat into shocks, and she was catching on fast. Before they left for the field, Mama told the wheat-harvest crew that dinner would be ready in a couple of hours, and she didn't want them to come in late because she was making fried chicken, mashed potatoes, gravy, and green beans. Then she added, "Thanks to Ed's new girlfriend, there will even be some sand plum cobbler for dessert." Ed couldn't quite figure out how Sasha could have had anything to do with it, but maybe Mama would tell them.

The harvest crew had a good start on the northeast forty by dinnertime, when their father called a halt to the cutting and shocking and said, "Let's go have some fried chicken."

They all agreed, and Ed said, "Well, the chicken will be good, but I'm really looking forward to the sand plum cobbler."

Bertha and Emma said, almost in unison, "I wonder why."

When they got to the house, their mother greeted them at the door with a washbasin of water and said, "Here, you wash up out here on the porch, and you won't get my house so dirty." She set the washbasin on a small table along with a small bar of lye soap.

The girls washed first, then the two boys, followed by their papa. And of course, Papa was the last one to the table. When he sat down, he immediately bowed his head and said, "Lord, we thank thee for this bountiful wheat crop we have just started to harvest. We ask thee for continued good weather until we have it all in. Keep us all safe as we labor in the field and here in our home. Bless this food to our nourishment and the hands that prepared it. In thy name, we pray. Amen."

As the food was being passed around, there were comments of how good it looked and then when they started eating, comments like, "Mama, this is delicious!"

When they were nearly finished with the chicken, potatoes, and gravy, Ed couldn't wait any longer and asked, "Mama, did you say you made some sand plum cobbler?"

"Yes, I did, son," Mama replied with a smile.

"Where did you get the sand plums?" Ed asked.

"Well, where do you think? When you were all out doing the chores this morning, I stepped outside just for a minute to check on my flowers. And right by the door, there was this bucket of sand plums, and on top of the plums was this note." She handed the note to Ed, saying, "I can't read English, but I did recognize one word." She pointed at it and asked, "Is that Sasha?"

Ed looked at the note and could hardly contain his excitement as he read it out loud. "I hope you have a good harvest. Sasha."

Then he translated it to the German dialect so his parents could understand it.

"What a sweet girl she is!" Mama said, adding, "And look at that beautiful handwriting." She held the note up so they could all see it.

Ed's heart was about to burst with pride for Sasha. Suddenly, he felt terrible when he realized she had to leave the plums secretly so his parents would not see that she was an Indian. *What a shame!* he thought.

"Mama, I promised Sasha I would bring her some cobbler the next time I see her. She has never had any. Will you save some for me to take to her?" Ed asked.

"I'll do better than that, Ed. I didn't use near all the plums today. I plan on baking a new cobbler later on in the week, so it will be fresh when you give it to her," Mama said.

"Thanks, Mama. That would be great. I love you, and thanks for this great dinner!" Ed replied with appreciation.

The rest of the family echoed Ed's thanks. "Yes, Mama. The dinner was great. Thank you so much!"

Their father stood up from the table and said, "Okay, everybody. It is time to get back to work so we get done by Saturday, and Ed can go see Sasha."

That afternoon, as they labored in the field, Ed kept thinking of Sasha. How did she get the plums to their front door without being seen? She almost had to arrive in the dark before all the morning chore activity began, hide someplace, and at just the right time, deliver them to the front door and sneak off without being seen. That would have been nearly impossible to do with the three of us men going this way and that, milking the cows, feeding the horses, feeding the sheep, letting the chickens out, and gathering the eggs. He finally decided if there was a way, Sasha could do it.

As the week progressed, a routine was established that allowed for the most efficiency. Everyone was up by five thirty each morning. The three men would go out to do the chores. Ed did the milking; Bill gathered the eggs, fed the chickens, and let them out of the coop. After the chickens were taken care of, he went to the sheep barn, fed the sheep, and let them out. Papa fed the cows and the hogs, and marveled each day how fast the pigs were growing. Finally, he went to the horse barn, fed the horses, and made sure they were in good condition.

The horses were not really needed for the cutting; but when the threshing started, they would be used to pull the wagon, hauling the wheat shocks to the threshing machine.

While the men were doing the chores outside, the two girls would be helping their mama with the daily chore of feeding a hungry harvest crew. As Mama would fix breakfast, Bertha and Emma would peel potatoes or whatever was needed for the noon meal she was preparing that day.

There was always bread dough to be made for the loaf of bread Mama baked fresh every day.

With that routine, everyone seemed to be finished with their daily chores at about the same time, and all were at the table ready for Mama's delicious breakfast. The fried eggs and bacon, pancakes and sausage, or biscuits and gravy were always there to start the day, but not before Papa would read a few verses in the Bible. He always included asking the blessing for the meal and thanking the Lord for continued good harvest weather and safety for his family.

There was no more talk at the table about Ed's new girlfriend, but that didn't mean he was not thinking of her almost continually during the day. He still had not figured out how she was able to deliver the sand plums to their front door without being seen.

The harvest crew was in the field daily by nine o'clock in the morning. They took an hour off for dinner, a twenty-minute lunch break at about four o'clock, and worked until about sundown which happened at about eight in the evening that time of year.

They had two minor harvest delays all week. On Wednesday afternoon, just when Mama arrived with sandwiches and lemonade for lunch, it showered lightly for about ten minutes. That day, Papa allowed thirty minutes instead of the customary twenty minutes for the lunch break to give the sun time to dry the straw out. It was not enough rain to make the wheat wet.

On Thursday, just when Mama arrived with sandwiches and lemonade for lunch break, Bill hit something with his scythe that made a chip in it so it would not cut right. Papa told him to go eat a sandwich while he repaired it. He was finished with it about the time his four kids were finished with their sandwiches. He told his wife he would skip the sandwich and just have some lemonade.

As she was pouring the lemonade, John said, "Hon, has anyone told you lately how lovely you look all dressed up for work like that?"

She almost spilled the lemonade as she handed it to her husband, put her hands on her hips, and said, "For land's sake, John! What's got into you to say something like that in front of the kids in the middle of harvest?"

John shrugged his shoulders and said, "It's true, and I just had to say it!"

Hilda couldn't help but join in the fun. "Come here, you big hunk!" she said as she grabbed her husband, cupped his sweaty face in her hands, and planted a kiss on his lips.

The four kids' jaws all dropped as they looked at each other in disbelief and whispered, "Can you believe our parents?"

Then Ed said to himself, "I sure hope I can be like that with my wife someday." Then he added, "And I sure hope it's Sasha."

"Okay, everybody, the fun is over. Let's get back to work," Papa said.

By Friday evening, at sundown, John estimated they had three or four acres of the barley left to cut. "What do you want to do? Cut it now or wait until tomorrow?" John asked his kids.

"Cut it now!" they all yelled.

"It will be dark when we get done!" John said.

"I'm not afraid of the dark, Papa, and Eddy wants to see Sasha tomorrow," Emma said.

"Thanks, Emma, for thinking of me. You're a little sweetheart, and you're sure a hard little worker," Ed told his little sister with an appreciative smile.

They all kept working until the barley was all cut and it was just about dark.

CHAPTER 10

The next morning, after the chores were done and they were just finishing breakfast, Ed asked, "Mama, may I take my Saturday night bath on Saturday morning this week?"

"Well, I should think so, son. I'm sure you need it just like the rest of us that have been working our tails off all week!"

Then he asked his mama, "Mama, did you have time to bake another sand plum cobbler?"

With a smile on her face, Mama answered, "Of course, I did, son. I baked a small one for you and Sasha, and a larger one for the rest of us. We will eat ours for supper, and you and Sasha can eat yours whenever. Do you want me to make a sandwich to take along again?"

"Would you please, Mama?" Ed asked.

Ed got the water bucket, took it to the water pump, and filled two kettles of water to put on the stove to heat up. Then he got four more buckets and poured them in the bathtub. He got a full set of clean clothes out of his room and hung them up on hooks in the bathroom. When the water in the two kettles on the stove was near boiling, he carefully poured the hot water into the bathtub, stripped off his dirty clothes, and crawled into the warm water. It was just right and felt so good.

Ed spent just enough time in the water to get clean, but not much more. He was so anxious to see Sasha again. When he had his clean clothes on and hair combed, he was ready to go.

Mama handed him the bag with the sandwich and cobbler, gave him a kiss on the cheek, and said, "Be sure to tell Sasha thanks for the sand plums. That was so sweet of her to do that."

"I will, Mama," he said as he grabbed his good hat and hurried out the door. He whistled at Copper, and he came trotting. He hadn't ridden him all week, and Copper was chomping at the bit to get going. Ed opened the gate and waited for him to step out of the corral, closed the gate, and swung unto Copper.

Copper seemed to know where they were going, so he headed toward the southwest corner of the pasture at a good gallop. Ed guided him around the cottonwood grove and then toward the stream. As he got closer, he could see Sasha sitting on one of the rock chairs by the stream.

When she saw him, she immediately got up and ran toward him. Grabbing his arm, she swung on behind him, threw her arms around him, and said, "I missed you, cowboy!"

He reached back, put one arm around her, and said, "I missed you too, Sasha. Where should we go?"

"Let's go to the stream. I brought a blanket along, and we can spread it out and sit on the grass," Sasha said.

When they got to the stream, Sasha slid off Copper's back. She got the blanket she had placed on one of the rock chairs, spread it out on the grass, sat down, crossed her legs, and beckoned for Ed to join her.

He sat down and crossed his legs, took her hands in his, and said, "It sure is good to see you again, Sasha. I missed you so much!"

She replied, "I thought of you every day and prayed you were having a safe harvest."

A little shyly, Ed told her, "I thought of you too, most of the day." Snapping his fingers, Ed remembered the first thing he was going to ask Sasha. "Sasha, all my family told me to tell you thanks for the sand plums, and we wondered how you left them there without us seeing you."

She giggled and said, "It sure wasn't easy. You are such a busy family. I really had to work fast to do it. When I left the farm where I live, it was still very dark. I ran most of the way to your farm so I would get there before daylight. I wanted your mama to find them, so I waited until all of you men came out of the house and started your chores. When I was sure none of you would see me, I ran up to the house, put them right beside the door, and ran as fast as I could to get behind the chicken coop before anyone saw me."

"You are such brave girl, Sasha. Mama was the one who found them when she went out to check her flowers. She was very impressed with your handwriting. It is beautiful, just like you," he said. "Mama made some cobbler for you and me. We will eat it for dinner."

"Will it be good with cold milk?" she asked.

"It will be delicious!" Ed said with a big smile.

"Sasha, last week, just before you got on Copper, you called me cowboy. And today again, you called me cowboy. What does that mean? Is it good or bad?"

Sasha withdrew her hand from his and softly caressed his cheek. "Ed, I did not mean to hurt you by calling you a cowboy. When I call you a cowboy, it means, 'a very good man,' because that is what you are, a very good man."

"Thank you, Sasha, but where did the word 'cowboy' come from?" he asked.

"Let me tell you," she said. "When I was still a little girl and before the Blue Coats came, ranchers in Texas would drive their cattle to, I think it was Abilene, Kansas. They had many, many cattle. They would drive them right across our land close to our village. Sometimes, some of the cattle would go right through our village and tear down our teepees, and the men driving the cattle would do nothing about it. There was one rancher that was better than all the rest. He stopped every year and would ask my papa how many steers we needed. If my papa said we needed three, he would give us three, then three more, and say those were for the other ranchers that did nothing for us. He was such a good man. Before he left, he always asked Papa if he could give me a ride on his shoulders. At first, Papa was not too sure about that. But then after the first time, he knew the man would never hurt me. The man would look at me and ask, 'Do you want to ride a horse?' I would nod my head, and he would say to me, 'Say, "Please, cowboy."' I would say, 'Please, cowboy,' and he would swoop me up, put me on his shoulders, and gallop around our village with me on his shoulders. I loved it, and you remind me of him, Ed. You wear a hat just like he used to, and you are kind to me just like he was."

"I'm glad not all white men have treated your people badly."

"So am I," Sasha said.

Ed looked up at the sun and was surprised how fast time went when he was with this pretty girl. He looked at Sasha and asked, "Are you hungry?"

"Yes, I can hardly wait to taste that sand plum cobbler," Sasha said with excitement.

"Me too," said Ed. He got up and went to the rock chair where he had placed the sandwich earlier. Sasha got the bottle of milk from the stream. It felt very cold. "Should we sit here on these rocks to eat?" he asked.

Sasha nodded and took the rock next to the stream. Ed sat down on the other one, bowed his head, and said grace in English so Sasha could understand what he said. "Dear Lord, I thank thee that you have brought me together with this beautiful girl who means so much to me. Bless our time together, and bless the food Mama has prepared for us. In your name, I pray. Amen."

Ed unwrapped the sandwich package Mama had made for him and was surprised to find two sandwiches inside. In one sandwich, there was what looked like a note wrapped up in the sandwich paper; Ed opened it first. He then opened the note, looked at Sasha, and said, "I think my mama wrote something to you, Sasha."

"Is it in German?" she asked.

"Yes, it is. I will read it first in German and then translate it to English for you," Ed said. After he had read it in German, he repeated it in English. "Sasha, Ed says you are such a sweet girl. I have said some terrible things about you that I have regretted ever since I said them. Can you ever forgive me? I look forward to meeting you someday soon. Ed's Mama."

Smiling, Sasha said, "Ed, tell your mama that I forgive her and hope to meet her someday soon also. And tell her, I think she has a great son."

Caressing her cheek with his fingertips, he replied, "You're so sweet, Sasha."

They both ate their sandwiches, and both agreed they were delicious. Then Ed got the cobbler out of the sack and showed it to Sasha. "Oh! That sure looks good," she said. "Look, Mama even gave us some little wooden forks to eat it with," Ed said.

"Your mama must be very thoughtful to think of that!" Sasha took the first bite of the cobbler and said, "Ed, this is delicious! How does your mama make it?"

"Well, I'm not sure," he said. "Should I ask her?"

"Yes, please do. I want to learn how to make it. I don't think Maria Regier has ever made any."

Ed was ready to change the subject, so he asked, "Sasha, are you happy living with the Regiers?"

"Oh, yes! They are good people, and they treat me right," she said with a smile.

"Does she make your clothes?" Ed asked.

"No, I make them," Sasha said.

"How do you make that? Isn't it from buffalo hide?" Ed asked.

Nodding her head, Sasha replied, "Yes, it is from buffalo hide. But I use cow hide, and it works just about as good."

"I like the way you look in it. I think you would look silly in a long cotton dress, like the Mennonite girls wear," Ed said.

"You should see me on Sunday when we go to church, because that is what I have to wear. Maria will not let me wear this buckskin to church. She says the people would talk."

Ed grinned and said, "They would probably talk about how pretty you look in it." Ed thought he saw Sasha actually blush a little when he said that. With a little hesitation, Ed asked Sasha, "Does Maria ever talk about making you into a white girl?"

With a hint of sadness, Sasha answered, "Yes, she did at first, but I told her I was Kancha and always will be Kancha. She said if I wanted to be Kancha, I would have to leave and go live with my own people when I turn sixteen. Then she said if after six months I wanted to come back and live as a Mennonite, I could, but then I would have to dress and live like Mennonites all the time. I don't know if I can do that."

Ed saw that she was about to cry and put his arms around her.

With tears in her eyes, she asked, "What should I do, Ed?" Then she broke down and started to cry like a small child.

Ed held her as close to him as he could. When the crying subsided a little, Ed asked, "When is your birthday, Sasha?"

"It is August 20," Sasha said, wiping tears from her face.

"That means in a couple of months, you have to leave," Ed said. The thought of losing Sasha made him want to hold her even tighter. "Where will you go, Sasha?"

"I don't know, Ed. There are so few of my people left anymore. I just don't know where I will go," she said, showing a bit of desperation.

Wrapping her in his arms, he reassured her that he would pray for her, adding, "I'm sure God will help you find some of your people."

"I'll pray too," she said.

The rest of the afternoon, they lay on the blanket in the sun and chatted about much lighter subjects. Watching the clouds float lazily in the sky, they imagined they could see different animals in the clouds.

The Regiers not making cobbler led them to the topic of what they did eat compared to the different foods that Ed's family ate. Then Sasha started talking about some of the things she remembered eating and doing with her biological family before they were all killed.

Ed was amazed by what Sasha remembered from only five years living with her biological family. A little later in the afternoon, Ed was again amazed at how fast time went by when he was with Sasha. In what seemed like just a few minutes, the sun had crossed the entire western sky, and Ed knew it was time for him to go home. He whistled at Copper, and he came trotting up to them.

Ed swung on first, looked down at Sasha, and said, "Would you like a ride, pretty lady?"

Giggling a little, she said, "Yes, I would, cowboy," then grabbed his arm and swung on behind him. Ed guided Copper over to the rock chair where Sasha had placed the milk bottle and the blanket. She swooped down and picked them off the chair.

"You're really good at that, pretty lady," Ed declared.

"I have such a handsome cowboy to help," she said as she threw her arms around Ed's waist and squeezed him tight.

Ed pointed Copper in the direction of the Regier farm and set him at an easy gallop. When they arrived at the spot just below the top of the hill, he stopped Copper and said. "This is where you get off, pretty lady."

Before she slid down, she asked Ed, "When will I see you again?"

"How about tomorrow, right after church?" Ed asked.

"Okay," she said. "Tomorrow, I will bring a picnic basket. Can you bring something to drink?"

"Do you like lemonade?" he asked.

"I love it!" she said.

With a big smile, he assured her he would bring the lemonade. "I will pick you up right here."

"I'll be waiting right here," she said as she grabbed Ed's arm and slid down.

He bent down, kissed the back of her hand, and said, "Goodbye, Sasha."

"Goodbye, Ed," she said, turning, and she ran over the hill. Ed watched her until she was out of sight.

CHAPTER 11

When Ed got home, it was obvious all the evening chores had been done already, so Ed guided Copper to the horse corral and let him into the corral. He threw down some hay for him, and then got the brush and brushed him down.

When he was about finished, Ed's father walked up, put his hand on Ed's shoulder, and asked, "How was your day today, son? I assume you and Sasha were together all day. Is that correct?"

"Yes, Papa. We were together all day. I really enjoy spending time with her. She is such a nice girl," he replied wistfully.

Standing with his arms crossed in a thoughtful pose, Papa stated, "It seems to me you are getting pretty serious about Sasha. You know your mama and I would really like to meet her, son."

Ed didn't know what to say now. They might want to meet Sasha, but Ed knew without a doubt they were not ready to meet her; and he wasn't sure they ever would be ready. "Maybe I'll bring her over one day, but I can't promise anything."

"That's fine, son. Whenever you want to bring her, we will be very happy to meet her. You know those sand plums by our front door sure softened up your mama about her. She has mentioned it to me several times how impressed she was that a girl would go to that much trouble to do something like that," Papa said with a smile.

Then Ed said, "Let me tell you something, Papa. Only Sasha could have done something like that. Do you know she ran most of the way over here in the dark carrying that pail of sand plums? Then she waited for just the right time so none of us would see her place the plums by the door. Then she hid behind the chicken coop until it was safe to leave without being seen."

"She must be quite a girl, all right!" Papa said. "Let's go eat supper, son. I think your mama is waiting on us."

Saturday supper most times consisted of bread pudding made from the leftover daily loaves of bread Mama baked every day during the week. Leftover bread was never as good as fresh baked bread, but throwing it out was not an option, so it was saved for bread pudding for Saturday supper. When the bread was made into a pudding, even bread several days old tasted very good.

Papa was the last to sit down at the table, so when he did, he bowed his head and said, "Lord, we are very grateful for thy bountiful love shown to us daily as we strive to do thy will. It appears the wheat will be a very good crop. We ask for continued good weather as we begin threshing it next week. Watch over us and keep us from harm as we labor together with our neighbors to get the wheat threshed. Lord, it seems Ed has found a girl that he enjoys spending time with. We pray that she is the girl you have chosen for him. Be with each of them as they get to know each other. Now we ask thy blessing on this food and ask that you bless the hands that have prepared it for us. In thy holy name, we pray. Amen."

After the bread pudding had been passed around, Ed said, "Mama, Sasha said the sand plum cobbler was delicious and that was the first time she had ever tasted it. She said Maria Regier has never made it, and she wonders if you would mind sharing your recipe with her so she could make it sometime for them."

Mama answered, "Son, I would be more than happy to share my recipe with that lovely girl. I'll get a piece of paper and write it down right now."

"Thanks, Mama. I'll translate it to English so she can read it." Ed could hear how pleased Mama was that Sasha wanted a recipe of hers.

Mama got a piece of paper and pencil, and began writing, and she then said, "I might have to think about this a little bit. I have never used a recipe. It is so simple. I just throw things together as I think of them." She wrote for a little while then stopped to erase a couple times and wrote again. After a few minutes, she said, "Here, son. I think this is everything I put in it."

Ed looked at it a little and then turned the paper over, and on the back, he wrote down in English what Mama had written in their German dialect. "Thanks, Mama. I'm sure Sasha will really appreciate this."

"Son, if Sasha needs anything from me, I mean anything, tell her that I will be happy to help her any way

I can. And son, I am so anxious to meet that lovely girl. When are you going to bring her over so your papa and I can meet her?"

"I'm not sure, Mama, but maybe someday soon," Ed answered cautiously.

"I hope so, son."

If Mama and Papa only knew, Ed thought to himself. Then Ed said, "Mama, Papa, today, Sasha told me something that really has me worried."

"What is it, son? What did she tell you?"

"She said the Regiers want her to do Rumspringa as soon as she turns sixteen. Papa, I don't even know for sure what Rumspringa is. Why do they do that, Papa?"

"Well, son, let me try to explain it to you."

"Please do, Papa."

"Some Mennonites feel they should let their children decide for themselves if they want to be Mennonite, so they let them leave and go live in the world any way they want. If they don't like that kind of life, they can come back and be Mennonites, and they believe they will be better Mennonites," Papa explained.

"I see," Ed said. "But why would anybody want to be anything but a Mennonite? Sasha said if she leaves, she is never coming back. Her birthday is August 20, so she will be leaving in just a couple of months. I will miss her so much."

Ed hoped he did not tell his parents too much. They might ask why Sasha was so sure she would never come back.

"Papa, I want you to know I have decided to give Copper to Sasha. I just can't let Sasha leave walking. That would not be right. She will be so much safer riding Copper, and I know Copper will take care of her.

Papa said, "Son, I am so proud of you. I know how much you love Copper and how hard it will be to give him up. But yes, it is the right thing to do. Like you said, she will be so much safer riding Copper than she would be if she would walk. But son, does Sasha know anything about horses? Does she even know how to ride a horse like Copper?"

Ed didn't know what to tell his papa. Most of the girls Ed knew could never ride a horse like Copper, and how could he tell papa that Sasha could probably ride as well as he could.

"Papa, trust me, Sasha is very good with horses!"

"Okay. I'll trust you, Ed. I just hope she doesn't fall off and get hurt," Papa said.

"No, Papa. I wouldn't worry about Sasha falling off and getting hurt. She is a very good rider."

Turning to Mama, he said, "I'm going to see Sasha again tomorrow after church. She is going to fix a picnic basket for dinner. I told her I would bring some lemonade to drink. Do we still have some lemons?" he asked hopefully. "I know you used a lot of them this past week for all the lemonade you brought out for lunch."

"Oh, I think I can still find enough lemons to make lemonade for two people," she assured him. She walked to a cupboard, looked in, and said, "Well, look here. There are six of them left. That should be just enough."

"Mama, you always say lemonade tastes better if you let it set awhile before you serve it. Would it be okay if we make it now?" Ed asked. Gathering the lemons and a knife to cut them, Mama replied, "You sure are trying to impress that lovely Sasha, son, but I'll go along with that. You go get some fresh water from the well, and I'll squeeze these lemons."

By the time Ed got back in the house with the water, there was one lemon left to squeeze. "Mama, let me squeeze that one so I can say I helped make it," Ed said.

"Okay, son. I'll get the sugar measured out. When you get all the juice out of that lemon, go down to the cellar and get that jug that is wrapped in burlap. We'll put the lemonade in there and then put it in the icebox until you are ready to go tomorrow after church. It will be nice and cold to go with that picnic dinner Sasha is making. Did she say what she will make?" Mama asked.

"Fried chicken, I guess. I don't know what else though," Ed answered.

Mama took a deep breath, let out a sigh, and said, "Oh, to be young again. When I think of all the picnic baskets I fixed for your papa to try and impress him."

"I bet they were delicious!" Ed said as he gave his mama a hug. "Thanks for your help, Mama. I'm going to bed now."

CHAPTER 12

In church on Sunday, Ed thought Rev. Schrag would never bring his sermon to a conclusion, and Ed was finding it difficult to sit still. He kept thinking about Sasha and the picnic basket full of food she would be bringing to their picnic this afternoon.

Finally, Ed heard the words he was waiting for, "Brothers and sisters, let us bow our heads for the closing prayer." As the congregation was leaving the church, it seemed like everyone had a special request or at least a story to share with Rev. Schrag as they were shaking hands with him at the west door of the church. Finally, when Ed's turn to shake the reverend's hand came, he would have liked more than anything to say, "See ya next Sunday, Reverend!" and be gone. But he politely got a good grip of the reverend's hand and said, "Good sermon. It meant a lot to me." Then he added, "Hope you have a good week."

"You too, son" Rev. Schrag said to Ed. Ed didn't like when he called him "son." He wasn't his son, and it was just an easy way to get by without learning the names of the younger people because he called most young people "son" or "daughter," whichever was appropriate.

On the ride home to the farm in the buggy, Papa looked at him and said, "I noticed the sermon was getting kind of long for you today, son."

"John, go easy on Ed. He is looking forward to his time with that lovely Sasha this afternoon," Mama said.

Ed could hardly believe his ears. His papa was getting after him, and his mama was defending him. It was usually the other way around, and if Mama only knew how "lovely" Sasha was with her black hair, brown eyes, and dark skin.

When they arrived at their farm, John let his wife and daughters off at the house and said, "Ed, you unharness the horses, and Bill and I will put the buggy away. When we get into the house, Ed, I want you to stay for the Bible reading, then you may go. And another thing, Ed, remember tomorrow we start the threshing of the wheat. Arnold Scott will have his threshing machine at the Jacob Albrecht farm tomorrow. That is where we will start. He will be ready to go by the time the dew is off the wheat."

"Okay, Papa. I'll be ready for the threshing," Ed promised.

Ed was surprised how short Papa's Bible reading was, and as soon as he was finished, Ed got up from the table and said, "Goodbye, everybody." He grabbed his good hat off the hook and headed for the door.

"Ed, aren't you forgetting something?" his mama yelled to him.

He slid to a stop, turned around, and said, "The lemonade!" He jogged back to the icebox and retrieved the lemonade. "Thanks, Mama, for reminding me!"

"Say hi to that lovely Sasha for us."

His two sisters added in unison, "Don't eat too much fried chicken."

Ed whistled at Copper when he was halfway to the corral, and of course, he came trotting to the gate. Ed opened the gate, and Copper stepped out and waited for Ed to swing on. But Ed needed to go into the barn to get the saddle bags he had made several years back. When he started riding Copper bareback most of the time, he made some saddlebags that worked well without a saddle to be tied to. They weren't much different than a regular set of saddle bags, only these Ed made to place in front of the rider instead of in back of the saddle. Ed added a piece of leather that he sat on to help hold the saddlebags in place. They worked best if both bags had about the same amount of weight in each one so they were balanced. Since Ed had just the jug of lemonade to place in one bag, he found a stone of about equal weight to place in the other side.

Finally, he was ready. He grabbed a handful of Copper's mane and swung on. He clicked his tongue and set Copper at a good gallop toward the southwest corner of the pasture. He slowed him down a little to go around the cottonwood grove and the plum thicket. He smiled when he thought how this exciting time in his life all started right there behind this plum thicket. When he got to the stream, he brought Copper to a stop and slid off. He got the jug of lemonade out of the saddlebag and put it in the stream to cool down. He swung back on Copper and walked him across the stream to the other side, clicked his tongue, and set Copper at a good gallop to the southeast to the hill where he expected Sasha to be waiting on him.

As he got closer to their meeting place, he could see that Sasha was not there yet. He was kind of surprised. This was the first time she was not waiting on him. Just then, he saw some black hair coming over the hill, and soon all of Sasha appeared. He noticed immediately that Sasha was wearing a different outfit today than any other day he had seen her. It was still buckskin, but something made this outfit more striking than the other one she had worn; and on top of that, she had tied a red ribbon in her hair. The red ribbon accentuated her black hair and dark complexion. Ed had always thought that a ribbon in the hair of a rather plain girl often did wonders for her, but a ribbon in the hair of a beautiful girl like Sasha was indescribable. To say the least, she was stunning!

"Hi, cowboy," she said as she got closer to Ed.

"Well, hi, pretty lady. How are you? You sure are pretty today!" Ed replied with a smile.

"You look pretty good yourself," Sasha said. "I hope you're hungry today."

"I'm very hungry today!" he said, rubbing his stomach. "Here, give me that basket then you can climb on behind me."

Sasha handed the basket up to Ed; and before he was barely ready, she grabbed his arm, swung on behind him, and squeezed him tightly. "It is sure good to see you, Ed. I missed you already, and we were just together last night."

"I missed you too, Sasha. Do you want to go back to the stream to eat?"

"Yes, let's go back there," she said. "I brought a blanket along so we can sit and eat."

Ed clicked his tongue and set Copper at an easy gallop. "What did you make to eat? I can smell it, and it is really making me hungry."

"I have five pieces of chicken: two drumsticks, two thighs, and a wishbone. Three pieces for you and two for me. What pieces do you like best?" Sasha asked.

"I like the drumsticks and the thighs. What do you like?" Ed asked.

"I like the wishbone and the thighs," Sasha replied. "Well, at least we won't fight over the wishbone. I also made some French fried potatoes, some biscuits, and a small cherry pie for dessert," Sasha said.

Ed replied, "Oh, that really sounds good! I made a jug of lemonade. Actually, Mama helped me. I have it in the stream, getting cold." As they neared the stream, Ed slowed Copper down to a walk and stopped him right by the stream.

Sasha took Ed's arm and slid down to the ground. Ed handed her the basket and slid down also. He helped Sasha spread the blanket out next to the stream and then went over to where he had placed the jug of lemonade. Picking it up, Ed said, "This should be good and cold by now."

Sasha sat down on the blanket and said, "Come on, Ed. I'm starving."

He sat down. He then took Sasha's hands in his and bowed his head, saying, "Dear Lord, we thank thee for this beautiful day. I thank thee for being able to spend this Sunday afternoon with this girl who means so much to me.

Bless our time together, and bless this food and the hands that prepared it. In thy name, we pray. Amen."

Sasha opened the basket, unwrapped the chicken, and handed a drumstick to Ed. "A drumstick for you and the wishbone for me. Here is a biscuit, and I even brought some honey butter that Maria made the other day. And here in this bag are the French fried potatoes," Sasha said.

"Sasha, what did you tell Maria you were doing with all this food?" Ed asked.

"I told her I was going to meet a friend. They have always given me a lot of freedom. They very seldom question where I have been or with whom. I always tell the truth, and they always trust me," Sasha explained.

"Sasha, that's good that you tell the truth, and they trust you," Ed told her. Pointing at her hair, he said, "I really like that red ribbon in your hair, but since today is Sunday, I'm a little disappointed you did not come in your long cotton Sunday dress."

Sasha burst out laughing. She gave Ed a make-believe punch on his shoulder and said. "Ed, you don't ever want to see me in that ugly dress. If you would see me, you probably wouldn't even recognize me in that thing. I look terrible!"

"Come on, Sasha," Ed said. "It can't be that bad."

"Oh yes, it can!" Sasha assured him.

"Did you have the red ribbon in your hair in church?" Ed asked.

"Of course not. Rev. Schroeder would have come down from the pulpit, yanked it out, and told me to leave," Sasha exclaimed.

"It's the same in our church," Ed said. Then he asked, "Do all the people in your church treat you nice? Has anybody ever tried to hurt you or say bad things about you?"

"All the people are very good to me. I have had some very, very good Sunday-school teachers. When the Regiers first took me to live with them, I did not know anything about the Bible or Jesus. They taught me a lot. Mrs. Siemens, my first Sunday-school teacher, taught me so much. Mrs. Ensz was another very good teacher who was kind to me and taught me a lot, and there were others," Sasha assured him.

"I can remember only one time since I have been living with the Regiers that someone was mean to me. It was in church just a short time after the Regiers rescued me. Rev. Schroeder was preaching about loving our neighbors. In the middle of the sermon, this man stood up, pointed his finger right at me, and said something like, 'Tell me, Rev. Schroeder, where in the Bible does it say we have to love a heathen like that?' Rev. Schroeder stopped his sermon and motioned for the elders to come up front. They had a short meeting, and then they went to the bad man, picked him up, threw him out of church, and told him never to come back unless he apologized to the church and to me. While they were throwing him out of church, everybody stood up, looked at me, and started singing 'Jesus Loves the Little Children of the World.' Ed, when that happened, I was still only five, maybe six, and I did not understand everything that had happened, but I knew Mennonites were good people,"

"We try to be good people, Sasha. But sometimes, we all sin and do bad things," Ed said, shaking his head. "Did the man ever apologize to you and the church?"

"Yes, he did. He got up one Sunday and went up to the pulpit, and in tears, said he was sorry for what he said to me. Then he came to me and hugged me, and said, 'Please forgive me for what I said about you.' I looked at Maria and nodded my head. She said, 'Sasha forgives you, and so do Samuel and I.' Today, this man's oldest daughter is one of my best friends," Sasha said, grinning.

"That is the way forgiveness is supposed to work," Ed said.

Sasha looked in the food basket and said, "There is one more piece of chicken here for you, cowboy."

"Sasha, the chicken was so good, but if I eat another piece, I won't have room for the pie. How about I save it for later?" Ed bargained.

"You want some pie now?" Sasha asked.

Ed nodded and said, "I love cherry pie!"

"Oh no," Sasha exclaimed. "Ed, I forgot to bring some forks to eat the pie with. I knew we could eat the chicken and French fries with our fingers, but I forgot about the pie!"

"No problem, pretty lady. Pie can be eaten with one's fingers also."

Laughing, Sasha said, "Here you go, cowboy. Use your fingers." Sasha held up the pie plate for Ed, and he gingerly took one piece out and took a bite.

"This is absolutely the best pie I have ever tasted!" Ed exclaimed.

Sasha took the remaining piece and took a bite. "I am surprised," she said. "It is much better than I expected. This is the first pie I ever baked!" When they finished the pie, Sasha said, "Ed, I almost forgot we have to break the wishbone!" She held it up for him and said, "Make a wish, cowboy."

Ed knew that the way Sasha was holding the wishbone, she would be getting the longer piece; thus, her wish would be the one to come true. He closed his eyes, made a wish anyway, and took hold of the wishbone. They both pulled. The rarity of rare happened. Both round pieces broke off the flat piece, and it fell to the ground. They were each left holding what would have been the short piece. Both their jaws fell open, and they both said together, "That never happens!"

Ed said, "I think that means God will decide if our wishes come true, not the silly wishbone."

Smiling, Sasha agreed, "I think you're right, Ed, and I like that better anyway."

"Me too," said Ed.

When the wishbone breaking was over, Sasha started to clean up everything and placed it in the basket.

Ed said, "Sasha, that was a great dinner. You are a very good cook. May I kiss you for fixing such a delicious meal?"

"Of course, you may kiss me, Ed. You may kiss me anytime you like. I like it when you kiss me." She held up the back of her hand for Ed to kiss.

For a moment, Ed was a bit puzzled, until he realized this beautiful girl who seemed so intelligent and confident had never seen a man and a woman kiss before. The only kiss she knew was a kiss on the back of her hand like Ed always gave her when she slid off Copper to go home. "No, Sasha. I mean a real kiss."

"That isn't a real kiss?" she asked.

"Well, not exactly. Let me show you what a real kiss is," he said. He gently drew Sasha close to him, cupped her face in his hands, and gently kissed her on the lips.

When Ed finished kissing her, she pulled back, blinked her eyes, and said, "I really like that kind of kiss, Ed! You may kiss me again like that." This time, Ed put his arms around her, squeezed her tightly, and kissed her with more passion.

"That was even better!" she exclaimed. "Can we do it again?"

"Maybe we should leave it at that," he said. This was the first time Ed realized how innocent this beautiful girl really was. He had always thought of her as intelligent, assertive, and the most confident girl he knew. "Sasha, don't the Regiers ever kiss like that?" asked Ed.

"I don't know. Not in front of me, they don't. I have never seen them kiss," she said uncertainly.

"What about your mama and papa? Did they ever kiss like that?" Ed asked.

"I think maybe, they did," she said. "But I was so young at the time I didn't know what they were doing, and I just forgot about it."

"Didn't your friends, your girlfriends, at school ever talk about kissing the boys?" he asked.

"No, not that I remember," Sasha replied.

Then Ed thought, *Well, if kids never saw their parents kiss, how were they supposed to learn?*

Sasha looked at the stream they were sitting right next to. She took off her moccasins, stuck her feet in the stream, and lay down on her back on the blanket.

"Ed, this really feels good! Come join me."

"You don't need to ask this cowboy twice!" he said as he pulled off his boots and socks, lay down right beside Sasha, and took her hand in his. The rest of the afternoon, they spent relaxing with their feet in the water, watching the clouds drift by and wishing they could stay that close to each other forever. Like always, when they were together, the time seemed to fly by. Before they knew it, the sun was setting.

With regret, Ed said, "Sasha, I have to go home." He whistled at Copper, and he came trotting up to them. Ed placed the bags on Copper and swung on. Sasha handed him the basket, grabbed his arm, and swung on behind. "Are you ready, pretty lady?" he asked.

She squeezed him tightly to let him know she was ready. He set Copper at an easy gallop toward the Regier farm, about two miles away.

As he brought Copper to a stop just below the crest of the hill, Sasha took Ed's arm and slid down. She pulled her hand away from his before he was able to kiss the back of her hand like always.

"You have to give me a real kiss this time, cowboy," she said smiling.

"You mean you don't mind?" Ed asked. He slid down from Copper, took Sasha in his arms, and kissed her passionately. Before he let her go, he said, "Sasha, I had such a wonderful time with you this afternoon. I wish we could do this every day. But tomorrow, we start threshing wheat. That will probably take about three weeks. After that, I will have to help Papa with the plowing to get the ground ready for the crop next year. I think Sunday afternoons are the only time I can see you, but I will think of you every day."

"Okay, Ed. I will think of you every day that we are apart, and each Sunday, I will bring a picnic basket," Sasha promised. With a smile, she asked, "Can you bring something to drink?"

"Yes, I will bring the drink, and I will pick you up right here," Ed promised. "Sasha, if it rains so we are not able to thresh, I will come see you. I will come right here and whistle very loudly for you. If you are able, will you come see me?" he asked.

"Of course, I will, Ed," she exclaimed.

"Okay. I will meet you here next Sunday after church." He took Sasha in his arms and kissed her again. Then he said, "Goodbye, pretty lady."

CHAPTER 13

Ed waited until Sasha was out of sight over the hill before he swung onto Copper and headed for home. When he got home, he could tell all the evening chores had been done already; so he put Copper in the corral, fed him some hay, and brushed him down a little. When he was finished, he headed up to the house. The rest of the family was just finishing supper when Ed walked in.

"We were wondering about you, Ed," Mama said. "Are you hungry, son? Can I fix something for you?"

"No, Mama. I am fine. Sasha brought a lot to eat, and I sure don't need anything more, but I would like to talk if we could."

"Sure, son. What do you want to talk about?"

"Well, I'm not sure, but you probably know already that I really like Sasha. Whenever I let her off to go to her home, I have always been kissing her on the back of her hand. Today, after we ate the large picnic dinner, I told her it was a very good dinner, and I asked if I could give her a kiss to thank her for it. She held out her hand for me to kiss. I told her I wanted to give her a real kiss, and she asked if that wasn't a real kiss. I told her not exactly. I took her in my arms, kissed her on her lips, and told her that was a real kiss. She said she liked it but had never seen anybody kiss like that before. I asked, don't the Regiers kiss like that? She said she had never seen them. I asked if her girlfriends at school never talked about kissing boys. She said they never did. Mama, Papa, don't those Mennonites believe in kissing?"

His papa winked at him and said, "Well, son, if they don't, they are sure missing out on some fun entertainment. Don't you agree?"

"John, shame on you!" Hilda chided.

"Hilda, what did you do the other day out in the wheat field? You kissed me. Now tell me the truth. Wasn't it at least a little fun?"

"Okay, okay. You will never let me forget about that. But you have not answered Ed's question, John."

"Well, I don't exactly know. To tell the truth, I have never seen any of them kiss their spouse. That doesn't mean they don't kiss at home in private. Listen, Ed, let me put it like this. They may feel that a kiss is something special that you share only with the one you love, and they feel no one should see it."

"Okay, Papa. So if kids never see their parents kiss, how would they learn how to kiss?"

"I don't know, son. You make a very good point."

"Papa, I'm sure happy I see you kiss Mama all the time. I think it is good that you do that in front of us kids. There is not a better way to show us that you love our mama. Papa, we have to know that you love her. If we didn't know that you love Mama, we would be afraid that any day, you might leave, and we could become orphans."

John got up, went to his son, and hugged him tightly. "Remember, son, I love your mama with all my heart. And I would never, ever leave her, and I love you and your brother and sisters very much also!"

"Papa, Mama, we all love you very much also."

John went to his wife and told her, "Hilda, I really do love you. You are the best wife any man could ever have." He took her in his arms and kissed her passionately. Then he said, "I think it is time we go to bed. We have a very busy week ahead."

"Night, Mama. Night, Papa."

"Good night to you too, son," they both said.

The next morning, they were all up at five thirty and got the chores all done much like when they were cutting the wheat. John got the team hitched to the flat wagon and parked it by the house until they were ready to go.

Today, Mama made biscuits, sausage, and gravy. This was Ed's favorite breakfast. He was actually the first one at the breakfast table, which rarely happened. Papa came in last because he was checking the team over and wanted to make sure everything was just right with the horses.

Finally, he came in, washed up, sat down at the table, bowed his head, and said, "Lord, we look forward to the coming weeks of threshing out our crop. Keep us all safe as we work around the machinery. Keep us in good harmony with our neighbors as we work together. Put aside petty disputes and jealousy that some may have. We ask thy blessing on this food and bless the hands that have prepared it. In thy holy name, we pray. Amen."

After the biscuits, sausage, and gravy had been passed around and they all started eating, Ed was the first to compliment his mama on the delicious breakfast. "Mama, this breakfast is great. The biscuits just melt in your mouth, and the sausage is so tender and tasty."

The other kids all joined in with, "Yes, Mama, this is a great breakfast!"

After they had all finished, Papa said, "Well, my two sons, we better get on the road to the Albrecht farm so we are there when the dew dries off the wheat shocks." He got up, went to his wife, and said, "Hilda, this was a great breakfast like always. I know I don't say it enough, but I really appreciate all you do for this family. You literally hold us all together. You and the girls have a good day, and remember, I really love you." He kissed her and said, "We will see you this evening."

CHAPTER 14

John and his two sons were on the road with the team and wagon shortly after sunup. The Albrecht farm was about seven miles away, so it would take almost an hour to get there. Jacob Albrecht was one of the larger farmers in the community. He owned two quarters, an eighty and a forty. Of course, it was not all tillable ground. His home quarter was all tillable, except where the homestead was, and he had wheat on all of it.

The adjoining quarter to the south of the homestead was mostly pasture, and he had it stocked with nearly a hundred sheep along with about twenty head of Texas longhorn cattle. It was rumored that he came by the cattle slightly illegal over time.

In early years, the Chisholm Trail passed just to the west of his farm. Jacob always needed water for his sheep, so he dug a pond in Crooked Creek and built a dam, thus insuring that his sheep had water even in the drought years.

In those same drought years, the cattle coming up the Chisholm Trail also needed water, and the drovers herding those cattle would sometimes let their herd of one thousand head or more of cattle help themselves to Jacob's water. That many thirsty cattle could drink a pond dry in no time at all. Being an upstanding member of the New Land Mennonite Church, Jacob was not going to deny water to thirsty animals, but he also was not going to just let them drink all the water they wanted for nothing. He would go to the trail boss and ask for just a couple of steers for retribution for his water. Sometimes, the trail boss was not in the mood to give some Kansas sodbuster some steers to pay for the water his herd drank; so the next night, Jacob and his eight sons would help themselves to one or two steers. Jacob claimed it was only fair, and it kept his family in beef. The question was if Jacob was only taking one or two steers for payment of the water, and using them for beef, where did the herd of twenty steers he had come from?

When John and his two sons arrived at the Albrecht farm, Arnold Scott, the steam engine and threshing machine owner, was well on the way to getting the steam built up in the steam engine so it would run the threshing machine. Jacob came over to the wagon, shook hands with John, and thanked him for coming and also for bringing his two good-looking boys. He told John that Harry Graber would be coming with his team and wagon, and Paul Schrag would be there also. Then he told John what part of the field to pick up first because he thought it was the driest and told him that it may be just a little damp yet, but by the time he had a wagon load, it should be okay; so he could go ahead and get started.

John clicked his tongue and slapped the reins on his team's back to get them started and guided them out to the field. When they were at the field, Ed and Bill jumped off the wagon with their pitchforks in hand and started pitching the shocks of wheat onto the wagon as their papa guided the wagon between two rows of wheat shocks.

Within just a few minutes, Harry Graber arrived with his team. He had just one son that was old enough for this hard work, so James Albrecht, one of the younger Albrecht boys, jumped on the wagon to help Robert Graber with the loading of that wagon.

Paul Schrag had just one son old enough to load the wagon also, so Harold Albrecht helped Willy, Paul's son, load their wagon. The other six Albrecht boys helped handle the grain as it came off the threshing machine. Two of the boys were bagging the grain as it came out of the machine. Two were loading and unloading the grain in the granary. One was driving the team pulling the grain wagon, and the youngest Albrecht boy, Keith, was the water boy. Although he was the youngest, and it was almost always customary for the youngest to be the water boy, his job was almost the most important job of all. He had to make trip after trip with two water buckets to the well to keep feeding the steam engine water to be made into steam. Without water, there was no steam; and without steam, there was no power to run the threshing machine.

Ed and Bill pitched the wheat shocks onto the wagon at a good pace. When they reached the far end of the field, the wagon was about half full already. This was ideal because it meant by the time they reached the home end of the field, the wagon would be full, and they could drive up to the threshing machine to unload the wheat shocks into the machine.

The first few times any team pulled the wagon beside the loud threshing machine was often a challenge for the one driving the team. Horses are naturally frightened by loud noises, and this machine definitely made a loud noise. As John guided his team toward the noisy threshing machine, they became skittish while still a good distance away from the machine. John knew from the way Ed had Copper trained that he was a much better horseman than he was, so he handed the reins to Ed and told him to take over. As soon as Ed took the reins, the team calmed down, and Ed guided them within a foot of the machine with no problem at all. As soon as he got the wagon parked and the brake set, the unloading crew jumped on to unload the wagon.

It was preferred by Arnold Scott that the same men unload all the wagons. It was very important that the wheat was fed into the threshing machine at an even rate. If the same men did it all the time, they soon learned how much capacity the machine had and also learned to feed the wheat into the machine evenly. The unloading crew was Bob Stucky, his brother Emil, and Ed Kaufman. This also allowed for the ones loading the wagon to take a short break and get a drink of water while their wagon was being unloaded.

While Ed was getting a drink, Jacob Albrecht came to him and said, "Hey, young man, I saw the way you handled that team of horses. Would you mind staying here and drive each team up to the machine the first few times? I think after a couple of times, the teams will get used to the noise and won't cause their owners any more problems.

I have one boy that isn't doing much for a while that can take your place loading your wagon. I already checked it out with your papa, and he said it was okay with him."

Ed said, "Yes, sir. I would be happy to do that."

The owners of all the teams were very grateful for Ed's way with horses. Each team was very frightened of the steam engine and threshing machine. But when Ed took the reins, there was something about him that was transmitted to the teams that they understood and were calmed down, and they were willing to do just as he asked of them.

Ed didn't know himself what it was, but he figured it was probably his calm demeanor that the teams understood and were willing to do as he asked. Some of the owners became skittish and nervous, just like their team, as they approached the steam engine. The team immediately could feel that in their owners, so they became even more nervous.

By the time the teams were guided to the loud machinery the third and fourth time, they were used to the noise and did not give their owners any more trouble, and Ed was allowed to go back to loading his papa's wagon.

The wheat yield was measured in bushels per acre. At the threshing machine, the farmers always put the wheat in bags because that was the most efficient way to handle the grain in those days. Each bag on average held five bushels of wheat. So if a farmer got four bags off one acre of wheat, his wheat yielded twenty bushels per acre, which was the average yield for the Turkey Red Wheat in Kansas in 1884.

Jacob Albrecht was rumored to tell his boys who were bagging the wheat as it came out of the thresher not to fill the bags too full. This meant there would be more bags to handle, but it also meant that it would appear that Jacob Albrecht had better wheat than most of his neighbors. For a proud man like Jacob, this was important.

At noon, all threshing operations shut down for about an hour so the ladies could feed the hungry crew dinner. This in itself was probably a more organized operation than what the threshing actually was. To feed fifteen to twenty hungry men and do it in an hour was no small task. It took a lot of fried chicken, roast beef, pork chops, or what the wife of the farmer whose wheat was being threshed on that particular day decided to feed the hungry crew. The young girls, who always came along with their mamas, had a lot of potatoes to peel and vegetables to get ready to cook.

Usually, tables were set up outside; and in most cases, there would be makeshift tables because few homes had that many tables, or that much room inside to feed that many people at once. When all the food was on the tables and all the men had been seated, the owner would get up and thank everybody for coming, maybe tell a short story or something, and then offer the blessing for the food.

About every other day, Arnold Scott had to move his machinery to the next farm. Several years ago, he decided that he would do the farms in alphabetical order. One year starting with Albrecht and ending with Zerger. The next year, Zerger would be first and Albrecht last. He also made it clear there would be no exceptions to this rule, and anybody who did not like it would be welcome to go somewhere else to get his wheat threshed.

Arnold was not a Mennonite, but married a Mennonite girl a few years ago and converted her to his faith, a Baptist. He enjoyed working with the Mennonites, but always said if he lived to be a hundred, he would never figure out what made Mennonites so competitive.

Doing the threshing in alphabetical order often times was not the most efficient because sometimes, the next one on the list lived several miles away; and there were neighbors just a mile away that needed their wheat threshed, but they were farther down the alphabetical list. To do the threshing in alphabetical order sure saved on arguing and bickering about who would get the machine next.

CHAPTER 15

Several times during the threshing days, it looked like they would get rained out; but the clouds always seemed to move around where they were working, and the threshing was able to continue. They worked every day, except Sundays of course, for three weeks straight without a rain delay. This was very unusual, and as was typical of farmers, they were becoming concerned how dry it was getting.

As was expected without a rain delay, and most assuredly hoped for the threshing to be finished in three weeks. The last bundle of Christian Zerger's wheat was run through the threshing machine a couple hours after the dinner break on Saturday.

When the last bundle of wheat was through the machine, Arnold Scott, like always, took off his straw hat and ran it through the machine. Some of the farmers did the same with their hats; others just threw theirs into the air. To say the least, they were all happy that year's harvest was over.

Ed would have been a little happier if they would have finished earlier in the day so he could have gone to see

Sasha yet that day. The way it was, he knew that by time they got home, it would be too late for that, but he could sure look forward to seeing her the next day.

On the way home, John figured his team was about worn out after three weeks of steady work, so he held them at a slow trot all the way home. He told his two sons sitting on each side of him in the wagon seat how proud he was of them for the hard work they put in every day. As they rode along, they chatted about the past three weeks' activities.

John asked his boys, "Which farm did you like working the best?"

There was a moment of silence, then Bill said, "I like the Carl Stucky farm the best."

"Why did you like that one the best?" his papa asked.

There was a moment of silence again before Bill finally answered his papa. "His youngest daughter, Anna, sure is pretty!"

John looked at Ed and exclaimed, "Listen to your younger brother. He is looking at girls already. Do you think he is old enough for that?"

Ed hesitated a little and said with a grin, "Well, Papa, I think he is old enough to look."

Their papa laughed and then asked jokingly, "What am I going to do with you boys?"

When they got home, Bill helped his papa unhook the team, unharness them, put them in the corral, and brushed them down as they munched on their oats and hay. Ed got Bessy and Erma in the barn and started milking them.

When John and Bill were done with the horses, they hurriedly did the rest of the chores.

When the chores were all finished, John announced to his two sons, "Boys, supper may not be quite ready yet, but since this is Saturday evening and we are all finished with the harvest, let's go in and relax a little before supper."

Ed exclaimed, "I'm all for that, Papa!"

Bill said, "Me too."

When the three men walked into the house, Hilda looked up from mashing potatoes, looked at John, and asked uncertainly, "Why are you in so early, John? Is something wrong? Supper is not ready yet."

John looked at his two sons, grinned, and said, "Look at your mama boys. She won't even let us relax a little on Saturday evening even when the harvest is all finished!"

"Come here you, big hunk," Hilda said as she wiped her hands on her apron and then went to her husband, gave him a big kiss, and said, "You get washed up, go sit in your chair, relax a bit, and supper will be ready in just a few minutes."

Bill said, "Mama, I'll wash my hands and set the table for you."

Ed asked, "What are we drinking, Mama? I'll make some lemonade, if that is okay."

"Thanks, boys," Mama said. "The lemons are in that cupboard on the east wall."

With all that help, in just a few minutes, Mama announced that supper was ready. John wanted to say grace, so he made it a point to get to the table last.

As soon as he sat down, he bowed his head and began, "Dear Lord, it is with humble gratefulness that we come to thee this evening. We have been blessed beyond measure with thy bountiful love toward us. By thy grace, we were given a wonderful harvest and great weather to get it all in safely. We were all protected from injury the whole harvest. There was little bickering and fighting between the neighbors, and all worked with one accord. For all this, we are most thankful. Now we ask thy blessing on this food and the hands that prepared it. In thy name, we pray. Amen."

CHAPTER 16

As he had done the past several weeks, when they got home from church, Ed's papa asked that Ed stayed for the Bible reading; and after that, he was free to go see Sasha. So as soon as Papa finished reading the Bible, Ed got up from the table and said, "I'll see you all this evening."

Then he got the drink, that was peach water this week, out of the icebox, grabbed his good hat off the hook, and was out the door. He whistled at Copper as he approached the horse corral. Copper came trotting to the gate. Ed opened the gate and let Copper step out, then closed the gate and went into the barn to get the bags to carry the jug of peach water to their picnic place. Ed grabbed a handful of mane and swung onto Copper's back. He clicked his tongue, and Copper was off at a good gallop in the right direction with no guidance at all from Ed. He knew where they were going.

Ed stopped Copper at the stream so he could place the jug of peach water in the stream to cool down and then swung back onto Copper to go to their meeting place.

As he approached the hill, he saw that Sasha was already there waiting for him. He could hardly believe his eyes when he saw what she was wearing. She had on a pair of buckskin pants with a buckskin top that had fancy leather strings hanging down, and of course, she had a red ribbon in her hair. Ed had never seen a girl in pants before, and he liked what he saw.

Sasha greeted him with, "Hi there, cowboy. How do you like my new outfit?"

Ed was a bit tongue-tied looking at Sasha, but he finally was able to spit out, "I love it, Sasha! You are the prettiest thing my eyes have ever seen."

"Thanks, cowboy. You look good yourself. Did you get finished with the harvest?"

"Yes, we did, and it sure feels good to be done with that! What's for dinner today, pretty lady?" Ed asked.

"I made fried chicken, and I have the usual pieces that you and I like. I also have freshly picked carrots and cauliflower from the Regier garden with sour cream, and you know what I have for dessert, cowboy? Mulberry pie!"

"Did you say mulberry pie? Give me that basket. I'm going to eat that pie right now!"

Sasha giggled and hugged the basket. She started to walk back over the hill and said, "I'm not going to let you have any because I like it too."

Ed slid off Copper, ran to Sasha, turned her around, kissed her passionately, and said, "Come on, pretty lady. Let's go eat. I'm hungry."

She said, "Me too."

Sasha handed Ed the basket and trotted over to Copper. In one smooth motion, she swung onto his back, looked at Ed, and said, "Would you like a ride, cowboy?"

"May I please, pretty lady?"

"Yes, you may, cowboy. Hand me the basket and climb on behind."

Ed handed Sasha the basket, grabbed her arm, swung on behind, and said, "I hope you know how to guide a horse like Copper."

"Watch me, cowboy," she said and clicked her tongue. She turned Copper around and headed him at a slow, easy gallop toward the stream where they always ate.

"You're pretty good at that, Sasha. How did you learn to ride like that?"

She turned around to look at Ed, giggling, and said, "I was born riding a horse."

"Well, that must have been a bit uncomfortable for your mama," Ed said, laughing.

"Honestly, Ed, I always watched how you did it, and that is what I've been doing, and Copper obeys me. He is sure a good horse!"

"Yes, he is," Ed agreed.

When they reached the stream, Sasha slowed Copper down and walked him through the stream. Ed slid off and took the basket from Sasha so she could slide off too. Copper walked a few steps where the grass was tall and lush, and started grazing.

"He will be happy all afternoon there," Ed said. He looked at Sasha and said, "Let's eat!"

Sasha got a blanket out of the basket, spread it out beside the stream, set the basket on the blanket, and sat down. Ed got the jug of peach water out of the stream and sat down in front of her, took her hands in his, and bowed his head to pray. "Dear Lord, I am truly blessed to have such a beautiful girl to share this Sunday afternoon with me. Bless our time together and bless this food that she has prepared for us. In thy name, we pray. Amen."

Sasha got the bag of chicken out of the basket and gave a thigh to Ed, then took one for herself. Ed took a bite of the chicken and said, "Sasha, you look absolutely gorgeous in that outfit. Surely, you wore it to church this morning, didn't you?"

Sasha was just taking a bite of her piece of chicken when Ed said that and almost choked on it when she started to laugh so hard.

"Are you plum crazy, cowboy? If I would have worn this to church, the elders would have picked me up and thrown me out of church like they did that man who called me a heathen that time!"

"You are probably right, Sasha, but I still think you look very pretty in it. And with that red ribbon in your hair, you are something else. Tell me, did you make it?"

"Yes, I made it. The Regiers butchered a steer a while back, and I saved all the hide. I made buckskin out of it and made both the pants and the blouse from the hide of the steer."

"You are very talented, Sasha," Ed commented. "I would not know where to begin to make something like that.

"Thanks, Ed. You are always so kind to me."

As Sasha was finishing the wishbone and Ed the drumstick, Sasha asked, "Are you ready for a piece of this mulberry pie, cowboy?"

"Yes, I am, pretty lady. Did you bring some forks this time, or do I have use my fingers again to eat the pie?" Ed asked jokingly.

Sasha reached into the picnic basket, pulled out two wooden forks, and held them up for Ed to see. "Say please, cowboy."

Ed leaned over a little to get a closer look at the two forks Sasha was holding and said, "Those look exactly like the two forks I brought to eat the sand plum cobbler with a few weeks ago."

A little defeated, Sasha said, "I figured you would recognize them, but I looked all through Maria's kitchen and I could not find anything except regular silverware forks. I was a little hesitant to bring some of those in case they got lost, so I washed these and put them away in case I need them sometime."

"That's okay, Sasha. Just because they are wooden, doesn't mean we can't wash them and reuse them."

Ed reached up his hand and was going to take one of the forks, but Sasha pulled it back and said, "No no, cowboy. You have not said please yet."

Ed batted his eyelashes at Sasha, took her other hand, kissed it, and said in a pleading voice, "Pretty please, pretty lady."

Sasha started giggling and said, "A real kiss would be even better, cowboy!"

Ed put his arm around Sasha and gently drew her closer to him. He gave her a passionate kiss on the lips. When he finished, he grinned and said, "All that for one little piece of pie!"

Sasha said, "I think you will like the pie. I had so many mulberries that I made a pie for the Regiers also. They gave me a piece of it, and it was very delicious."

Sasha got the pie out of the basket, placed a piece on a tin plate, set one of the forks she was still holding beside the pie, and handed it to Ed. "Here you go, cowboy. I hope you like it."

Ed waited until Sasha had her piece on a plate also, and they both took a bite together. "This pie is awesome," Ed exclaimed.

Sasha nodded her head as she was swallowing her first bite and said, "I agree with you, Ed. It is delicious!" As they were both scraping their pie plates clean, Sasha asked, "Ed, would you like to go for a walk this afternoon?"

"Sure, Sasha. Where do you want to walk to?"

Sasha hesitated for a moment then said, "Ed, I would like to show you where I was born and where I lived until I was five years old. Would you like to see it?"

"Sasha, are you kidding? I would love to see it! How far is it? Do we walk, or do we ride Copper?"

"It is about three miles. I would like to walk," she said.

"Me too!" Ed said.

Sasha finished putting everything in the basket and put the basket on the rock chair. She took Ed's hand, and with her other hand, she pointed to the southwest and said, "It is in that direction. Follow me, cowboy."

After they crossed the stream, Sasha started running. Ed hoped she was not going to run all the way because he didn't think he could run that far.

In a while, they came to another stream and slowed down to a walk to cross it.

Sasha pointed out to Ed that this was the same stream they ate by. It had a fork in it, and one fork went west. The fork they just crossed went to the southwest.

Sasha said, "We are about halfway there now. Are you getting tired, cowboy?"

"No, I'm fine," Ed said. "Let's run some more."

Sasha took off running again, and Ed ran along with her. In a while, Sasha slowed down to a walk. "I'm tired, Ed," she said.

"So am I," Ed admitted.

"Where I used to live is just over the next hill. We can walk the rest of the way."

When they topped the hill, Ed was in awe of what he saw. There were a few scattered remains of what used to be tepees. In the distance, there was a row of about thirty large crosses with a space separating them in about half and half. In front of the large crosses, there were ten smaller crosses.

Sasha squeezed Ed's hand and said, "Come," as she gestured with her head toward the crosses. Ed followed her. When they reached the crosses, Sasha immediately kneeled down, and her body began to shake as she cried uncontrollably. Ed knelt down beside her, put his arm around her, and held her tight. They stayed like that for several moments.

In a short time, Sasha stopped crying and got to her feet. She wiped her face with her hands, looked at Ed, and said, "Thanks for holding me, Ed. You are always so kind to me."

Then she explained, "Ed, about five years after all these people were killed, Samuel and Maria brought me here to show me this. Samuel said the day after they rescued me, about twenty men from their community came back to bury all these people. The men are on the right, and the women are on the left. That gap in the crosses separates the men from the women. These ten small crosses are where they buried the children. He apologized to me that they were not able to identify anybody because they knew nobody. I thanked him over and over for doing what they did. If the Blue Coats had done it, they would have dug one big hole and have thrown everybody in it. This is so much better. I try to come here about every year to repair any of the crosses that are broken and need repair."

Ed hugged Sasha and said, "You are an amazing girl, Sasha. Your mama and papa would be very proud of you." Then Ed said, "Look, Sasha, in the west, at that cloud. It is really going to rain pretty soon, and we will get very wet."

Sasha whispered to Ed, "Give me one moment please." She knelt down, made a steeple with her hands, and placed them in front of her face. Ed bowed his head, folded his hands, and stood right beside Sasha. In a moment, Sasha stood up and mouthed, "Thank you!" to Ed, took his hand, and said, "We have to go." They took off running.

Before they were out of the area that used to be the village, the rain was pouring down in sheets, and there were lightning flashed everywhere.

Sasha yelled at Ed, "I know an abandoned house where we can take shelter. It is not very far."

Ed yelled back, "Let's go there!"

108

Sasha turned slightly to the west and continued running.

Shortly, Ed could make out the outline of a small square house in the distance. "Is that it?" he yelled.

"Yes, that is it, but the door to get in is on the far side," Sasha yelled.

Ed just nodded his head the best he could in all the rain and wind.

When they got to the house, Sasha led the way around to the far side, found the door, turned the handle, opened the door, and walked in. Ed just stood there, looking at Sasha in amazement.

"Are you just going to stand there and get all wet, cowboy, or are you going to come in and build a fire so your girlfriend can get warmed up?"

"Well, what's wrong if I stand here and just look at you because you look so good all soaking wet like that? But I'll come in and build a fire just for you. Is there actually a stove and firewood in here?"

"Yes, Ed. There's the stove, and there is some firewood back in the corner over there in the box, and I think there are some matches in one of those cupboards."

Ed went over to the stove to see if it was safe to build a fire in it, and then he looked at Sasha and asked, "How did you know about this place, Sasha? Have you been here before?"

"Yes, I've been here many times. When I was a little girl, there was a kind older man and woman living here. They had kind of a store here. People from my village would come here to trade for things that we did not have.

I remember my papa would bring deer meat, coon, and beaver skins—just about anything. And the people here would give us coffee or sugar, salt and pepper, or anything we needed. I remember one time my papa even brought me a rag doll to play with. I loved that doll.

"Ed, are you going to build a fire? I'm getting cold in these wet clothes."

"Yeah, so am I," said Ed. "I'll have a fire going here in just a little bit. Sasha, I want you to take off those wet clothes because you might get sick being so wet and cold for so long."

"Ed, I can't take off all my clothes in front of a young man like you. What kind of a girl do you think I am anyway?" she asked with a big grin.

"Sasha, I...I...didn't mean that the way it sounded. Can you find me a rope or a long piece of wire and a bedsheet or something like that, and I'll fix it so you can take your clothes off and I won't see a thing."

In a few minutes, Ed had a good fire going in the stove, and it began warming up the one-room house.

Sasha came to where Ed was warming himself by the stove. She was carrying what appeared to be a long rope and two bedsheets.

"That is just what I need, Sasha." Ed looked up at the ceiling, and there just happened to be a nail in the ceiling about a foot from the stovepipe. Ed took one end of the rope and tied it to the nail. On the other end of the room, right above the door, there was some kind of a hook. Ed took the other end of the rope, pulled it tight, and tied it to the hook.

He looked at Sasha and said, "Now we will hang those sheets over the rope, and you will have your private room, and I will have mine. We can take off our wet clothes and hang them up close to the stove, and maybe by morning, they will be dry."

He had barely said that when Sasha placed her wet blouse over the rope. In a moment, her pants were over the rope also. Then she said laughing, "You know, Ed, ever since that first time I saw you looking at me behind that sand plum thicket, I have dreamt of spending the night with you, but not necessarily in separate rooms."

"Shame on you, Sasha!" Ed exclaimed.

"What, Ed, you never dreamed of spending the night with me?"

"Yes, I did, Sasha. Many times. But in the Bible, it says, 'Thou shalt not lust.'"

"I know. I'm sorry, Ed."

Ed thought he heard Sasha rummaging through some stuff, and he asked, "What are you doing, Sasha?"

She replied, "There is a very small closet back here, and I actually found a robe for me. I was looking for something for you so we can eat supper together in the same room. All I found for you is a very large towel that you can wrap around your waist." She slid the towel under the bedsheet to Ed.

"This towel fits me fine, Sasha, but I heard you say something about supper. Do you expect me to go out and shoot a deer or something in a towel! Besides that, I don't even have a gun."

"No, cowboy," Sasha said, giggling. "There in the corner by the wood box, if you look closely, there is a trap door. It goes down to a cold room, and I have a slab of bacon wrapped up very tightly in paper, and there are several jars of beans that Maria canned and let me bring over here. Sometimes, when I come here to work on those crosses for Mama and Papa all day, I get hungry, so I can come here and have something to eat. There is a frying skillet down there also. Be sure to take the lantern with you because it is very dark down there."

Ed found the bacon, beans, and skillet just like Sasha said. He took the bacon and beans to the door, laid them up on the floor, went back to get the skillet, and climbed back out. When he got out, Sasha had the bacon on a cutting board and was slicing it already.

"How many pieces do you want, cowboy?" Sasha asked.

"I'll take two, maybe three," Ed said thoughtfully.

"Okay, cowboy, here is what I will do. I will slice and fry five pieces for you and four for me because what we do not eat for supper, we'll save and eat in the morning for breakfast."

"That is a good plan, pretty lady. And by the way, you look very lovely in that robe. It fits you perfectly."

"You look good in that towel, cowboy, but I sure hope it does not fall off."

"Me too. I was a little worried climbing up and down that ladder to the cold room, and with both hands occupied, I would have been in trouble."

Sasha giggled as she wrapped the slab of bacon back up tightly in the paper and handed it to Ed to take back down to the cold room.

When he got back up, Sasha had all the bacon in the skillet, and the aroma of fried bacon was filling up the small house.

"Sasha, you are making me awfully hungry with the smell of bacon."

"Just be patient, cowboy. The bacon will be nice and crisp in a few minutes, and then I'll heat up the beans and we will be ready to eat. If you open that cupboard up there," she pointed up to her right, "you'll find two tin plates and cups. And I think there are even two forks up there also."

Ed opened the cupboard and found everything just as Sasha said there would be. "But what are we going to drink, pretty lady?" he asked.

Sasha put her hands on her hips, looked at Ed with a stern face, and said, "You expect me to provide everything just like your mama always does."

Ed had never seen that look on Sasha before. He put his hands up, jumped back a little, and blurted out, "No no, Sasha. If there is nothing to drink, that is just fine!"

Sasha started laughing hysterically. She went to Ed, put her arms around his neck, and gave him two short kisses on the lips. "I'm sorry, Ed. I didn't mean to show you how mean I can be. I was just joking," She kissed him again and said, "If you go outside by this corner of the house, there is a downspout. I always keep a large pot under there to collect rainwater. It may not be very clean, but we will boil it, and it makes great coffee. I'll get the coffee pot ready while you get the water."

Ed went out and found the large pot full and running over. He took it inside, and Sasha found a dipper and dipped water from the pot into the coffee pot. "We can start eating now while this boils a while."

There was a small table and a chair on Sasha's side and a chair on Ed's side, so he picked it up and took it to the table on Sasha's side. Sasha placed three pieces of bacon in a plate for Ed and two in the other plate, and then she spooned several large spoonful of beans into each plate.

"Supper is ready, cowboy. Let's eat."

Ed went to Sasha's side of the small table, pulled out the chair for her, and gestured for her to sit down. He then helped her move the chair closer to the table, and he went to his side, pulled the chair out, and sat down. He took Sasha's hands in his and bowed his head to pray. "Dear Lord, I thank thee so much for this amazing girl that thou hast blessed me with. She means so much to me. I thank thee for thy protecting care over us during this storm. Be with us tonight as we sleep. Now I ask thy blessing on this food. Bless the hands that have prepared it. In thy name, we pray. Amen."

Sasha picked up her fork, smiled at Ed, and said, "Ed, you are such a gentleman. That was the first time in my life that anybody ever helped me to be seated."

Ed didn't quite know what to say. "You are such a pretty lady, Sasha, and a man should always help a lady, pretty or not. This is such a delicious supper, Sasha."

"You helped, Ed."

Then with a concerned look on her face, she said, "Ed, I'm worried about Copper. Do you think he is okay? Is he still where we left him?"

Ed said, "Sasha, don't worry about Copper. He is fine. He has been in many storms in his life. When it started raining, he probably walked to that grove of cottonwood trees and spent the night there. In the morning, if it is not raining anymore, he will probably come look for us."

"Ed, do you really think he will come look for us?"

"I would almost bet on it, Sasha. That is just the way he is. They call it instinct."

"Yes, he has great instinct," Sasha said. "But I'm still worried about him."

"He'll be okay," Ed assured her. "Are you ready for some coffee, pretty lady? I think it is ready. I'll get us some." Ed got up, found a hot pad by the stove, and brought the pot to the table. He filled Sasha's cup, then filled his own.

Sasha said, "Thank you, Ed. It sure does smell good."

"Yes, it does," Ed agreed.

They both sipped their coffee slowly. Ed was not a big coffee drinker, but he could not ever remember drinking a better cup of it.

Sasha asked, "Ed, was it still raining when you went out to get the water before supper."

"Yes, it was, but not nearly as hard as this afternoon when we got here. There was still a lot of lightning in the west, so it may rain all night," Ed said. Then he asked, "Sasha, what are we going to sleep on? Are there some blankets some place that we can lie on the floor, so we don't have to sleep on the hard wood floor?"

Sasha grinned at Ed and said, "The old couple that lived here was well prepared for the cold Kansas winters. I found six heavy blankets back there and two very nice pillows, and even with pillowcases on them. Can you believe that?"

"Wow, this will be just like sleeping at home. Sasha, if you want to make our beds, I will wash the dishes. How would that be?"

"Thanks, Ed. You are such a gentleman. I'll be happy to fix our beds."

Ed got up from the table, kissed Sasha, and said, "Thanks for the great supper, Sasha." Then he pulled her chair out slightly as she stood up.

She turned around, threw her arms around his neck, kissed him, and said, "Thanks for being such a good gentleman to me, Ed."

"You're welcome, Sasha."

Ed gathered up the dishes. There was no sink to wash them in, so he brought the pot of water to the table. After throwing the remaining coffee out the door, he washed the coffee pot first and filled it with fresh water. He washed the tin cups, the tin plates, and last of all, the forks. He found a towel to dry everything and placed them in the cupboard that he took them out of earlier. When that was all done, he took the large pot outside to the downspout where there was still a lot of water coming out. He rinsed the pot out good and set it under the downspout. He was sure it would be full and running over again by morning.

When he got back in the house, Sasha had both beds made. For each bed, she had two blankets stacked up, one on top of the other one. The third blanket on top folded back right below the pillow. Ed was amazed how neat it looked and how inviting also. He was tired and ready for bed.

Sasha said, "Ed, I just turned all our clothes over. They were dry already on top but still a little wet underneath. By morning, they should be nice and dry."

"Thanks, Sasha, for doing that. I'll place the lantern right here where we can both reach it if we need to, and when you're ready, I'll turn it out."

In a moment, Sasha said, "I'm ready, Ed. You can turn it out. Good night, cowboy. Sleep tight."

"You too, pretty lady. Sleep tight, and I'll see you in the morning."

CHAPTER 17

Ed was awakened when he heard Sasha say, "Hey, cowboy, time to wake up. What would you like for breakfast, bacon and beans, or would you rather have bacon and beans?"

Ed laughed and said, "If that is all you have, I would rather have bacon and beans."

"Well then, get up and get dressed because I'm not going to let you come to the table dressed the way I think you are dressed."

"How can I get dressed with you standing there watching me?"

"Ed, I promise not to turn around and look, although it would be very tempting," she said, giggling.

"Sasha, what did I tell you just yesterday about lusting?"

"I'm sorry, Ed. I don't think I'm lusting. Doesn't it also say something about tempting other people? Didn't Jesus tell Satan not to tempt him?"

Ed was completely dressed already. He tiptoed up behind Sasha and put his fingers in her sides to tickle her. She jumped, screamed, and turned around. She then threw her arms around Ed and kissed him.

"I think you're the one tempting somebody when you look so beautiful in the morning, pretty lady. How are you today? Did you sleep well?"

"I'm very good, Ed, and slept great. Now if you get those tin plates and cups out of the cupboard and set the table, we will be ready to eat in just a couple of minutes."

Ed did as he was told. He barely had the table set when Sasha was there with the coffee pot, filling the cups with coffee. She returned the pot to the stove and came with the skillet to fill their plates. Ed waited behind her chair, pulled it out for her, and helped her to be seated.

"Thank you, Ed. You are such a gentleman."

Ed went to his chair, sat down, took Sasha's hands in his, and bowed his head to pray. "Dear, Lord, we thank thee for thy protecting care over us as we slept so peacefully. We thank thee for this day. Be with us as we return to our families. Help them to understand that we did nothing sinful last night. Now we ask thy blessing on this food. In thy name, we pray. Amen."

Sasha said, "Ed, I broke up all the bacon into little pieces and mixed it up with the beans. I always think reheated beans never taste very good, and the bacon helps a lot to make them taste better. I hope you like it like that."

"Sasha, that was a great idea. This is a great breakfast. You are a wonderful cook. When you went out to get the water, was it still raining?"

"No, Ed. Not at all. In fact, it was clear in the west. In a few hours, the sun should be shinning."

"Sasha, what are you going to tell Samuel and Maria why you did not come home last night?"

"Ed, I told you one time I always tell them the truth, and they always believe me. I will tell them that after my friend and I ate the picnic dinner, I wanted to show my friend where I used to live and where my parents are buried. We then got caught in a storm, so we had to spend the night in this house. They will understand. Ed, are you going to tell your parents you spent the night with me?"

"Yes, I will have to because they know I came to see you yesterday, but they will wonder why I did not come home when I saw it was going to rain. I cannot tell them that we went to see where you used to live because they do not know that you are Kancha."

"Ed, you have never told them that I am Kancha? They think I am a white girl?"

"Yes, Sasha. They think you are a white Mennonite girl."

"Ed, are you ashamed of me because I am Kancha and not a white Mennonite girl."

Ed was shocked that Sasha would even think that he was ashamed of her being Kancha. "Sasha, you know that is not true! You are the most beautiful girl I know! I could never ever be ashamed of you! You mean more to me than anybody in the world!"

Sasha wiped some tears from her eyes and said, "I know, Ed. I'm sorry I asked you that. I should never have done that."

Ed said, "That's okay, Sasha. I understand."

Just then, there was a loud horse whinny from just outside the door. Ed and Sasha both got up and ran to the door. Ed opened the door, and Copper was about to walk into the house.

Ed and Sasha both yelled, "Copper." They both threw their arms around his neck and hugged him. He nuzzled them both like old friends that they were.

Ed said, "I told you, Sasha, that he would probably come look for us in the morning."

"How did he know we were in this house?" Sasha asked.

"Some people call it instinct. But I still think Copper is a very smart horse."

"I agree with you, Ed," Sasha said.

"He probably wants to go home already. We should go clean up this place, leave it the way we found it, and go home," Ed said.

They went back into the house. Copper would have followed them inside if Ed would have let him, but he told him to wait for them and they would be ready in a few minutes. Copper obeyed Ed and waited right by the door.

Back inside, Ed volunteered to do the dishes, and Sasha said she would take up the beds and put them away. Then they both took the sheets down, making it a one-room house again. Ed untied the rope and coiled it up while Sasha folded the sheets and put them away. Ed checked the fire in the stove. It was about out, and he threw the remaining water that was in the water pot in the stove and that pretty well put out everything.

"I think we are ready to go, Sasha. I'll put this pot under the downspout, and it should be full the next time it rains."

Copper was still waiting for them just outside the door. Ed put the pot where it belonged, and then came and swung unto Copper. Sasha was right behind him, and Copper was off at a nice, easy gallop.

When they got to the first stream, it was not the small clear stream they were used to seeing. It was about three times as wide and came up just past the bottom of Copper's belly at the deepest place. Ed had to lift his feet just a little to keep his boots out of the water.

When they were across it, Sasha asked Ed, "Do you think Maria's picnic basket will still be on that rock where I left it, or did the water carry it away?"

"I don't know, Sasha. I'm sure the water got very close to it. We will know in just a few minutes."

As they got closer to the stream, Ed could tell Sasha was trying to look over his shoulder to see if the basket was still on the rock.

"I can't see it, Sasha. I'm afraid it is gone. It looks like the water almost covered the rock up so it sure would have floated the basket away."

"Ed, Ed, turn Copper over there." She pointed to the south. "Way over there. What is that yellow thing?"

"It looks like a basket to me, Sasha."

Ed set Copper at a gallop toward the yellow object, nearly a quarter of a mile away. The closer they got, the more it looked like a basket. Ed guided Copper right beside the basket. Sasha took hold of Ed's arm, reached way down, and picked it off the ground.

"Look at it, Ed! Not a thing wrong with it! Can you believe that?"

"You know what happened, Sasha. You remember yesterday just before it started to rain, the wind was blowing so strong from the north. The wind blew the basket off the rock and way over here. If it had stayed on the rock, the water would have floated it away. I think God loves you very much, Sasha, and he said, 'I'm going to save that basket for that beautiful girl.'"

Sasha said, "Thank you. Thank you, God, for saving Maria's basket."

Ed set Copper at an easy gallop to the hill where he would let Sasha off. He brought Copper to a stop just below the top of the hill, and Sasha slid off. Ed slid off also, took Sasha in his arms, and kissed her passionately. Then he grinned and said, "Sasha, I will always remember our first night together. You were a perfect lady."

Sasha said, "Ed, you were a perfect gentleman. Not for one minute was I afraid that you might do something bad to me. You are such a wonderful man."

Ed kissed her again and said, "Goodbye, Sasha. May I see you again next Sunday?"

"Bye, Ed. See you next Sunday."

Ed swung back onto Copper and watched until she was out of sight. He turned Copper and set him at a good gallop headed for home.

Ed wondered what kind of trouble he would be in when he got home. There was absolutely no doubt in his mind that Sasha or he did anything wrong, but would he be able to convince his parents of that?

He slowed Copper down to cross the creek where they always ate. Just after they crossed it, Ed saw something sticking out of the mud a few feet away. He rode Cooper closer and then recognized it as his saddlebags. Worrying about Sasha's picnic basket, he completely forgot about the bags.

They were two heavy for the wind to blow away, and when they got full of water, they wouldn't even float away. He slid off Copper to get the bags. They were totally covered in mud. He took them back to where the water was and washed the mud off the best he could. He was hoping when they dried out, he could get some more of the mud off.

He carried them back to where Copper was waiting and said, "Sorry, Copper. You might not like these bags as wet as they are, but we don't have too far to go." He placed the bags on Copper's withers. He didn't seem to mind too much, so Ed swung back on and clicked his tongue. They were back at a good gallop toward home.

Copper stopped at the gate. Ed slid off to open up the gate and let Copper walk in. Ed went up the hayloft to throw some hay down for Copper. He got the brush and brushed him down good, then headed to the house to face his family.

When he walked in the door, his parents, brother, and sisters were all sitting around the table. There was no food on the table, so he was not quite sure why they were at the table. They all got up and came running to Ed. Everyone hugged him all at once and welcomed him home. This definitely was not the homecoming he was expecting.

Finally, Papa said, "Son, we were all sitting around the table and were getting ready to pray for your safe return.

You had us all so worried, and we are all very thankful that you are back home. But I think you owe us an explanation on where you have been for the past almost twenty-four hours."

"Papa, can we all sit back down. I want to tell you all what happened." They all went back to their chairs at the table.

Ed said, "I'm very thankful to be back home safely. After Sasha and I finished eating our picnic dinner, she asked if we could go for a walk. She wanted to show me an abandoned trading post her papa used to take her along to when he went there to get some supplies. She said it was about three miles toward the southwest from where we were eating.

"I suggested we take Copper, but she said she would rather walk, so we walked."

John interrupted his son to ask, "Ed, was that a rather smalls square building made out of sod, with no windows and just one door on the west side?"

"Yes, Papa, that's it. Have you been there?"

"Yes. I used to go there also to get some supplies. It was run by a nice older couple named Henderson. I wonder what ever happened to them. One day, they were gone, and no one seemed to know where they went, or what happened to them. Sorry to interrupt, son."

Ed continued, "We were in there for just a short time, and when we went outside to go back to our picnic area, the sky looked terrible. We started running, but before we went very far, it was raining so hard we could not see where we were. We decided it would be best to turn around and try to find the trading post again. We were able to find it, but we were soaking wet by that time. It kept raining until way past dark, and we did not want to walk in the dark.

"We found a long rope and some bedsheets that we hung up from one wall to the other to divide the room so Sasha would have her privacy, and I would have mine.

"There was a wood stove in there. I lit it so we could warm up. I told Sasha we should take off all our clothes and hang them on the rope close to the stove so they would dry out. I promised to stay on my side, and she promised to stay on her side. And we both kept our promises all night."

John looked at his wife, and he could see that she believed Ed's story. So John said, "Son, your mama and I have no reason to believe that you are not telling the truth, so we will believe you, but remember we have to keep this incident between this family only. We must not tell anyone!" He looked at his three younger children. "Do you all understand that?"

"If rumors get out that Ed and Sasha were together all night, it will ruin their reputation. They will have to apologize to the church, and that is always very difficult to do."

Ed was relieved that everybody believed him. He was expecting it to be much worse.

CHAPTER 18

Ed and Sasha continued meeting every Sunday afternoon. Her picnic basket would be filled with something different every Sunday. One Sunday, she even made a Kancha dish that she vaguely remembered her mama making one time. It was made mostly out of corn, so Sasha used some sweet corn that the Regiers raised. Along with that dish, she made some jerky out of some roast beef that she cut into strips and dried. Ed found the corn dish okay, but he loved the jerky. It was something he had often heard of but never had eaten before.

Ed's mama helped make different drinks to take to the picnic also. Along with the lemonade, he took watermelon water, cantaloupe water, peach water, and orange juice. All these drinks were made from produce they raised.

As the date of August 20 drew nearer, Sasha started talking more and more about it. As they lay on the blanket by the stream wrapped in each other's arms, Sasha would ask, "What am I going to do, Ed? Where will I go? How will I get there? I am so scared, Ed! Please tell me what to do."

One time, Ed answered her with, "Let's get married!"

Sasha abruptly sat up, looked Ed straight in the eye, and said, "Ed, don't you ever, ever say that again! You know I want to marry you more than anything in the world, but you know good and well we cannot do that. The Regiers absolutely would not allow me to marry you. Your parents would not allow you to marry me. My church and your church both would probably kick us out and tell us not to even try to come back. Ed, it just would not work, but I would marry you today in a heartbeat if we could!" Then she kissed him passionately to prove it.

As much as Ed and Sasha prayed and hoped that August 20 would never come, it did come. The day before, they were together most of the day. They reminisced a lot about the short three months that they knew each other. They laughed when they remembered that first time they saw each other behind the sand plum thicket.

"Why did you run away from me that first time after giving me that heart-melting smile of yours?" Ed asked.

"What was I supposed to do? I had never seen a more handsome man in my life. I was afraid you were a ghost or something and would attack me."

"And you didn't want to be attacked by the most handsome man you had ever seen?"

Sasha giggled and said, "Well, maybe just a little." Sasha then turned serious and asked, "Ed, will you ever regret that I came back to the plum thicket the next day, hoping with all my heart that you too would come the next day?"

"No, Sasha. I have never been sorry and never will be sorry that I went back the next day, hoping that you would be there. The time I have spent with you will have been worth it no matter how painful it will be for me not to ever see you again."

"Me too, Ed. I have enjoyed every minute I've been with you! My only wish would be that it would last forever, but I know now that is not possible. But I will always have a soft spot in my heart for you," touching her chest as she said it.

Ed had not yet told Sasha that he was giving her Copper to leave on so she would not have to walk. He knew that she would probably refuse to take him, so he had decided to tell her it was her birthday present from him.

Ed asked her, "Sasha, do you have a lot of stuff to take when you leave?"

"No, not really," she said. "All I'm taking are three dresses—that nice buckskin dress that I usually wear on Sundays, that pants suit I made just recently, and that horrible cotton dress that I wear to church—some water, and Maria said I can take all the food I want. I have made a lot of jerky out of roast beef that will last me several days."

"That's good, Sasha, because you are taking Copper with you. You can put all that in those saddlebags I have. That will be my birthday present for you."

Sasha replied sternly, "No, Ed. I cannot take Copper. He is your horse, and I absolutely will not take him."

"Oh yes, you will," Ed replied. "There is no way I'm going to let you leave, walking. It wouldn't even be right to do that."

"I can't, Ed!"

"Yes, you can, and there will be no more talk about it! Do you want the saddle and bridle, or just bareback without anything except the two bags?"

"I can't take the saddle too. I'm fine riding bareback," she said, choking back the tears. "Like always, you are so kind to me and such a gentleman. Thank you so much. That will make it so much easier for me, and I will feel so much safer riding Copper." She kissed Ed and gave him a big hug. "How can I ever thank you for that? I promise to take very good care of him."

"I know you will, Sasha, and that is all I ask. I'm sure I can find another horse and train him like Copper. Sasha, what time are you going to leave tomorrow?" Ed asked.

"I will say goodbye to the Regiers tonight before they go to bed. I want to leave about sunup. They never get up that early."

"Okay, I will meet you right here by the hill," Ed said. "I have to go home now." He took Sasha in his arms and held her tight for a moment. He then kissed her several times and said, "Goodbye, pretty lady. I sure am glad I taught you what a real kiss is."

"So am I!" she said. "Goodbye, cowboy!"

He watched as Sasha walked over the hill and was out of sight. How many times had he done that in the last few months, he wondered. This would probably be the last time. It almost made him cry to think about it. He finally made himself swing onto Copper and head for home.

When he arrived at their farm, he stopped Copper at the gate, slid down, opened it, and let Copper walk in. He threw down some hay for him and even got just a little oats that was actually for the workhorses when they were working hard. He put it in the trough beside the manger where the hay was. He got the brush and brushed him down. This too would be the last time he did that with Copper. When he finished, he put his arms around Copper's neck and said, "I'm sure going to miss you, old boy. We have been a lot of places together. Now I want you to watch over Sasha for me. I know you will do it, Copper, and I know she will take very could care of you."

Copper nickered just a little, as if he understood what Ed had said to him.

When Ed finally got to the house, everybody was at the supper table waiting for him. He went to the sink and washed his hands, then took his place at the table. He bowed his head and cleared his throat, but before he could start his prayer, his papa started with, "Lord, tomorrow will be the hardest day of our son's young life. Be with him and ease his pain of losing the one who has meant so much to him these last few months. Give him the strength to go on without her and bring someone new into his life in time. We also ask that you will be with Sasha. Protect her from all harm and help her find whatever she may be searching for. Now we ask thy blessing on this food and the hands that have prepared it for us. In thy name, we pray. Amen."

Trying hard to choke back his tears, Ed looked at his papa and said, "Thanks so much, Papa." Then he looked at his mama, and said, "I'm so sorry, Mama. The food looks so good, but I'm just not hungry. May I be excused?"

"Sure, son. It's okay. I understand," Mama said.

Ed got up, went to his room, and closed the door. He then lay down on the bed without even taking off his boots and cried. About an hour later, he got up, took off his boots and socks, removed his clothes, went back to bed, crawled under the covers, and tried to sleep. It was useless. Sleep never came for him that night. He finally got up and looked out the east window of his bedroom. He could tell it was time for him to get up and go meet Sasha for the last time.

He put his clothes on, and went to the kitchen sink to wash his face and comb his hair a little. He grabbed his hat off the hook and headed for the door. About halfway to the horse corral, he whistled for Copper, who came trotting to the gate. Ed let him step out then went to get the saddle-bags and placed them on his withers. He grabbed a handful of mane and swung onto his back. Copper knew where they were going and headed in that direction.

When they reached the meeting place just behind the hill, the sun was just peeking over the horizon. At about the same time, Ed could see Sasha's black hair come over the hill. When she got closer, Ed could see that she also had slept little or not at all that night. In fact, it looked more like she cried most of the night.

When she got close to where Ed was waiting with Copper, she tried to hide her face from Ed and said, "Ed, I can't let you see me like this!"

He grabbed her and said, "Sasha, it is okay. I look just as bad, if not worse!" Ed helped Sasha put the things she was carrying into the saddlebags. When they finished, Ed pulled her close to him and kissed her. Then said, "Sasha, trust in God. He will take you where you want to go."

She grabbed a handful of Copper's mane, swung on, and headed him to the west. Ed watched until Sasha and Copper were out of sight.

He started to walk home, but only took a few steps before he fell down in the dirt and cried like a baby. He had no idea how long he lay in the dirt crying; but when he finally pulled himself together and got up, the sun was quite high in the eastern sky. He slowly continued walking toward his home.

When he was about halfway home, the thought struck him that during all the times Sasha and he were together, not one time did either one of them ever say those three little words, "I love you." *Why not?* he wondered. He knew he loved her, and he was sure she loved him just as much. Then why did they never say it. He finally concluded that deep down, they both knew their love for each other was a forbidden love that could never be, so it was best just not to ever say those three little words, "I love you."

CHAPTER 19

The first two weeks after Sasha left were the worst days of Ed's life. It seemed he thought of her constantly all day long. He wondered where she was, if she was all right, what was she doing, was she still riding, searching for some of her people? Sometimes, those thoughts almost brought tears to his eyes. But he had decided he would not cry over her again. As time went on, the pain got easier, and he realized that there were times during the day that his mind was on something other than Sasha.

Then one Sunday after church, Ed was walking with his parents, his brother, and two sisters toward their buggy to go home and something like a miracle happened. A girl with golden blond hair and sparkling blue eyes came jogging up to them. She stuck out her hand, and when Ed took it, she said, "Hi, my name is Katrina, and my parents bought that Waltner place that has been vacant for some time. We just moved in last week, so I hardly know anybody. I would really like to go to that young people's social the church is having this Saturday that Rev. Schrag was talking about, and I need somebody to take me. I heard that you might be able to do that?" Her sparkling blue eyes were dancing, waiting for an answer from Ed.

Ed was flabbergasted by this girl's brave approach and was searching for words to say, when his sister Bertha said, "Ed, all you have say is, 'Sure, I'd be happy to take you.'"

Ed finally blurted out, "Sure, I'd be happy to take you. You said your parents bought the vacant Waltner place?"

"Yes, they did," she answered. "Do you know where it is?"

"Of course, I know where it is. It is practically in our front yard. We are next-door neighbors. I'll pick you up at five thirty," Ed said.

"Great, I'll be waiting for you."

As Katrina was rushing away, Bertha looked at her younger sister and said, "That Katrina is really a beautiful girl. Don't you think so?"

"Yes, I agree," said Emma. "She would be a real catch for somebody."

Ed was listening to his sisters, and finally, it dawned on him that maybe Katrina didn't do that on her own. He looked at Bertha, then at Emma, and said, "Did you two have anything to do with that?"

They both looked at each other, shrugged their shoulders, and said, "We don't know what you are talking about."

During the week, Ed found himself getting anxious for Saturday evening to arrive. He did his chores with more enthusiasm than he had in weeks. He even got the buggy out and cleaned it up so it would look good for Saturday evening. When Saturday finally arrived, he told Mama that he was taking his Saturday night bath on Saturday afternoon this week.

His mama just winked at him and said, "I'm so glad that you are getting back to yourself, Ed."

"So am I, Mama. I never knew I could hurt like that before, and I'm glad I'm over it now."

"That's good, son. We were all worried about you and praying for you every day."

"Thank you, Mama."

Before he took his bath, he got the team hitched to the buggy and parked it in front of the house. After Ed was finished with his bath, he put on some of his best clothes and combed his hair. He even went back to the mirror several times just to check if he looked okay. Finally, the clock on the mantle said it was a few minutes before 5:30 p.m. so he told everyone he was leaving.

His papa gave him a little hug and said, "Enjoy the social, son."

His mama hugged him, kissed him on the cheek, and said, "I hope you have a great time, son. Katrina really seems like a wonderful girl."

Bertha and Emma were waiting by the door and with sly grins on their faces. Each said, "Say hi to Katrina for me."

The buggy ride to Katrina's house took just a couple of minutes, so Ed barely had time to think what he would say to Katrina when he picked her up at her front door. When he got to her place, he parked the buggy so she would be able to step in, and he would follow her right in and be at the right place to drive the team. He got out, walked up to the door, and knocked. In just a moment, the door opened. Katrina stepped out and said, "Hi, Ed. It is so nice to see you again. How are you this evening?"

Ed answered, "I'm fine, Katrina. How are you? You look great!" She had on a light blue cotton dress with a white light sweater. She even had a blue ribbon in her hair to accentuate her blond hair. Ed wondered how she knew he liked a ribbon in the hair of a pretty girl. They walked down the sidewalk to the buggy. At the buggy, Ed took Katrina's hand and helped her in. When she was seated, he stepped up into the buggy, sat down beside her, took the reins, released the brake, clicked his tongue, and slapped the backs of the team with the lines lightly. They were on their way.

The church was about two miles away, and Ed kept the team at a very slow trot all the way. He wanted as much time as possible to get to know the pretty girl beside him. He soon learned that she was very easy to talk with. If Ed wasn't talking, she seemed very able and willing to fill in the silence, but it was not useless chatter just to be saying something. She seemed genuinely interested in learning about Ed and what he was interested in. She also seemed to be interested in her new home here in Kansas. She asked several questions about Kansas, and Ed was happy to answer them for her.

When they arrived at the church, there were a number of young people there already. It seemed most of them lived close enough that they were able to walk because there were only two other buggies there. Ed parked beside the other two, set the brake, stepped down, went to the front of the team, and tied them to the hitch rail. Then he went back to the buggy to help Katrina down. He held out his hand for her, and she took it with her right hand. With her left hand, she pulled up her dress slightly, so not to trip over it, and stepped down from the buggy gracefully.

Ed kept hold of her hand as they walked toward the church. The church really did not have a social room, so everyone was gathered outside, just in front of the church. There were several tables that were loaded with food of all kinds. There were also several containers of drinks available and a large bowl of punch.

Rev. Schrag and his wife Elfrieda were hosts of this affair. Later, Ed was surprised to learn that the cost of the food and everything came out of the reverend's pocket. He could hardly believe it.

When all of the young people arrived, Rev. Schrag welcomed them all and then had a short blessing for the food and the activities that followed. He told them to get in line and help themselves to the food, and he sure did not want to see any leftovers.

Ed looked at Katrina and asked, "Are you hungry?"

"I'm starved," she said.

Ed said, "So am I. Follow me." He took her hand and led her to the end of the food line. They filled their plates, then went and found some empty chairs beside some of Ed's close friends who were already seated with their dates, enjoying the food. When they were seated, one of Ed's closest friends said, "Hey, Ed, good to see you again. Tell us who the lovely lady is you brought with you this evening." Ed introduced Katrina as his new neighbor that just moved in last week all the way from Saskatchewan, Canada. Then he introduced each of his friends and their dates to Katrina. Katrina was soon chatting with the other girls like they had known each other forever.

When all had finished eating, Rev. Schrag got up and said it was time to play some games. Everyone was given a piece of paper and told to write on it three things about themselves that not everybody knew.

Ed wrote, "I was born in Russia, I have two sisters and one brother, and I once had a date with a girl who was from the other Mennonites."

When all the papers were handed in, Rev. Schrag started to read each one aloud, and everyone was asked to guess who he was talking about. A number of them had written they were born in Russia, and several wrote that they lived on a farm, but the clue that gave most of them away was when they wrote how many siblings they had.

When Rev. Schrag came to Ed's clues, he looked at it a bit then started with the last clue that said, "I once had a date with a girl from the other Mennonites." All the jaws dropped, and there were some "oh my and wows." Rev. Schrag said, "Well, we are sure happy it was just one date." Ed was happy he did not write the whole truth to that clue. The reverend went on to read Ed's other two clues, but no one was able to guess who it was, and Ed had to confess he was the one who had a date with a girl from the other Mennonites. Then some of Ed's friends wanted to know what it was like to date one of those other Mennonites. Ed simply said, "Try it sometime."

Katrina giggled a little, patted Ed on the back, and said, "Good answer, Ed."

Ed thought, *If they only knew who I dated, and not just once.*

When that game was over, the reverend led the group in singing some well-known hymns. Next, they played a game where they had to get up and move around a little, followed by more singing, and then the final game was questions about the Bible. Ed was amazed at Katrina's knowledge of the Bible. There were several questions that no one else knew the answer to, but she did.

There was one more round of hymn singing, and then Rev. Schrag said, "Ladies and gentlemen, I'm sorry to announce that if we don't close this party down, get home, and get to bed, there is a good chance that I may fall asleep during my sermon tomorrow morning.

That brought on cheers and laughter, and then a loud applause and a standing ovation from everyone. Rev. Schrag thanked them all for coming and promised to do it again real soon. The young men found their dates, if they were not still with them, and then everyone filed by the reverend and Elfrieda, thanked them for everything, and said they had a great time. Some of the young men, including Ed, went to Rev. Schrag and offered to help clean up.

"No no. This was for you, young people, and I'm not going to make you work for it. I have the trustees coming to help clean up."

Ed was holding Katrina's hand as they walked with some other couples to their buggies that were parked in the back. Everybody agreed it was a great social and hoped Rev. Schrag kept his promise to do it again soon.

When they arrived at the buggy, Ed helped Katrina in. He untied the team, climbed in, and sat down beside her. He released the brake, clicked his tongue, and guided the team toward the road and home. Ed was enjoying this evening so much he hated for it to end. He kept the team at a very slow trot. He and Katrina chatted and laughed all the way to her place.

When they arrived at her house, he parked the buggy and set the brake. He climbed out and took Katrina's hand, helped her out, and walked her to the door.

At the door, almost giggling, Katrina said, "Ed, will you ever forgive me for being so brash and asking you to take me to this social?"

Ed acted like he had to think about it for a minute, then said, "Yes, Katrina. I may forgive you if you promise to tell me what role my two younger sisters played in all of this."

"Oh, Ed, I have to tell you that you have the sweetest sisters anybody could ever hope to have. The younger one, Emma, she is just a doll.

"It was the day after we moved in that my papa asked me to trim some weeds along our driveway. I must confess, I was dressed for work and looked pretty bad. I had on the oldest, ugliest dress I have. My hair was a mess, and I looked terrible. But I was trimming some weeds, so who cares. I was close to the road when your two sisters came by singing, chatting, skipping along just as carefree as could be. That is, until they saw me. I must have scared

Emma half to death. She looked at me and asked, 'Who are you? You are not supposed to be here because this place is vacant.'

"I explained to her that we just moved in the day before. I told her my name was Katrina Gering. I had two younger brothers, Joe and Ted, and my parents were Victor and Elisabeth Gering. I said we moved here from Saskatchewan, Canada. Finally, she gave me a chance to ask her name. She said, 'My name is Emma Krehbiel. This is my sister Bertha. We have two brothers, Ed and Bill, and our parents are John and Hilda.'

"Then I said, 'With a name like Krehbiel, you must be Mennonites.' Just like that, she changed completely and got all excited.

"She said, 'Yes, we are. How did you know? Are you Mennonite too? Do you want to come to our church? Why did you move here all the way from Saskatchewan? What does your papa do? Is he a farmer?'

"I had to stop her from asking so many questions so I wouldn't forget what she asked before I could answer them all. I said, 'yes, we are Mennonites, and most likely the same kind of Mennonites as you.' I said, 'I would love to go to your church, but where is it?' She gave me perfect directions to get there and told me Rev. Schrag was the minister, and he was a good man. She even told me what time Sunday school and the service start. I told her we moved here from Saskatchewan because my mama has asthma, and the harsh winters in Saskatchewan were very hard for my mama. Papa hoped it would be better here in Kansas. I also told her my papa was a farmer, and he bought all the ground that belonged to the Waltner place.

"Then Emma said, 'I have one more question. Do you have a boyfriend?'

"Bertha scolded her and said, 'Emma, that is none of your business.'

"Emma was not going to give up that easily. She almost whispered to Bertha, but I could understand what she said. 'Bertha, she would be perfect for Ed.'

"I told her that I used to kind of have a boyfriend, but when we left Canada, I had to say goodbye to him. And it is all right with me if I never see him again.

"Emma said, 'Our older brother, Ed, had to say good-bye to his girlfriend several weeks ago, and he is still on the mend. He just cannot get over her. We think you should ask him to take you to the church social in a couple of weeks.'

"I asked her, 'Why should I ask him? He should ask me.'

"Emma said, 'Yes, that is the way it usually works, but Ed is still hurting so much he will never ask a girl for a date.'

"I asked, 'If he is still hurting so much, do you think he would take me if I ask him?'

"Then Bertha finally said something, 'If you ask him, we will see that he takes you.'

"I asked, 'How will I know who he is? I have never met him?'"

"Emma said, 'We always sit in the third bench from the front, on the right hand side of the sanctuary, and Ed always sits by Papa.'"

After this long explanation, Ed pretended to wipe his forehead with the back of his hand and said, "Whew! That sounds just like my little sisters, always looking out for their older brother. Since they went to so much trouble to get us together, may I ask to call on you again?"

"That would be lovely to have you call on me again, and I will be waiting for you."

Ed brought the back of Katrina's hand to his lips, kissed it softly, and said, "Goodnight, Katrina."

He waited until she was inside the house, turned, and walked to the buggy. He felt so happy his feet barely touched the sidewalk.

Ed called on Katrina frequently. They grew very close to each other in no time at all. As promised by Rev. Schrag, there were several more socials. A year to the day of Ed taking Katrina to the first church social, Ed proposed marriage to her. They were married a few months later, on October 11, 1886, in the New Land Mennonite Church. The whole church was invited.

CHAPTER 20

As was quite common in those days when a young man married, a room or two was built onto the house where the young man grew up, and the couple moved in and lived in the same house with his parents. This was the case with Ed and Katrina. By the time of the wedding, the two extra rooms were mostly finished.

About a week after the wedding, Ed and his papa were doing some finishing work on the outside of the two rooms that had been added when Ed heard a horse whinny. The sound came from the driveway. Ed looked that way and could hardly believe his eyes. He dropped his hammer and ran in that direction. There were two horses walking up the driveway ridden by a young couple. Ed recognized Copper immediately, but he had to look twice to recognize the slightly, more modestly dressed Sasha than what he was used to seeing.

As the horses got closer, Sasha raised her hand and said, "Hi, cowboy. It is good to see you again. How are you?" She slid down off Copper, ran to Ed, and embraced him. A few moments later, Copper came up to Ed and nuzzled him. "I think he is happy to see you and happy to be home again," Sasha said. Then she turned to the handsome young man still sitting on the other horse.

"Ed, I would like you to meet my husband, Solu. It means 'quiet water' in our tongue."

Solu slid down from the horse, came over to Ed, and said, "I am so pleased to meet you, Ed! Sasha has told me a little about you."

Ed extended his hand saying, "Come to the house. You both have to meet my family. Sasha, I must warn you, Mama may faint when she sees you, so be prepared."

Sasha giggled and said, "Do I actually look that much different than most Mennonite girls?"

Ed winked at her and said, "Yes, you do, Sasha, but that never bothered me much."

When they got to the house, Ed opened the door and said, "Mama, Katrina, we will have a couple of guests for dinner. Is that all right?"

He heard his mama say, "Of course, Ed. Have them come in. Who are they?"

Sasha and Solu stepped in, and Ed said, "Katrina, I would like you to meet a good friend of mine, Sasha, and her husband, Solu."

Before Ed could introduce Katrina, he heard his mama say, "Oh my Lord, I had no idea!" as she grabbed the kitchen door to keep from falling to the floor.

Ed ran to her to help keep her from falling and asked, "Mama, are you okay?"

Mama slowly gathered herself together, wiped her forehead with her apron, and finally said, "Ed, you never told me Sasha was…was…" she paused a moment, then said, "was so beautiful!"

Ed embraced his mama and said, "I think I did, Mama. Probably several times, and yes, Sasha is Kancha. I never told you because I was afraid of what might happen, and I think you just proved I was right."

His mama nodded and mumbled, "Yes, you are." She went to Sasha, embraced her, and said, "Sasha, I am so pleased to meet you. You made quite an impression on our Ed."

Ed noticed Katrina standing to the side, looking a bit perplexed at what she had just seen take place. He went to Katrina, put his arm around her, and said, "Sasha, I would like you to meet my wonderful wife, as of one week today, Katrina."

Sasha went to Katrina, embraced her, and said, "Katrina, I am so pleased to meet you." Sasha looked at Ed and said, "Ed, you have a very lovely wife. I love her blond hair."

Katrina, still a bit perplexed, smiled and said, "It is nice to meet you too, Sasha."

About this time, Papa, hearing the commotion inside, decided to check it out. When he walked into the room, Ed said, "Papa, we have some special guests. Papa, I want you to meet Sasha and her husband, Solu. Sasha, this is my papa."

Papa's eyes got big, and he said, "Well, I'll be," as Sasha went to him and embraced him. He looked at Ed and said, "I always figured Sasha was different in some way because you never brought her over and introduced her to us, but I had no idea."

Hilda came over, put her arm around her husband, and said, "Our son can sure keep a secret, can't he?"

"Well, I should say so!" John said.

"Come on, everybody. Sit down. Dinner is ready," Mama said, guiding them to the table. A couple of plates and chairs had already been added, so everybody was just a little closer together than was normal, but it was still very comfortable.

When everyone was seated, Sasha looked at Ed and asked, "Ed, may I say the blessing?"

"Yes, of course. Please do."

Sasha bowed her head and began in the perfect German dialect that was spoken in this house. "Dear Lord, I thank thee for bringing me to the house of this young man who has meant so much to me and has done so much for me in the past. I thank thee for finally being able to meet his wonderful family. Bless this day and our time together. Now we ask thy blessing on this food and bless the dear hands that have prepared it. We ask these things in thy holy name. Amen."

When she finished, Ed said in amazement, "Sasha, you never told me you speak our German also."

Smiling, she said, "I didn't until I met Solu, and he taught me to speak your German."

Surprised, Ed said, "Sasha, you have to tell us all about that right now!"

"I will, I will. First, let me get some of the delicious dinner your mama cooked into my tummy. I'm about starved."

Everyone was silent for a few minutes as they began to eat. In a few minutes, Sasha picked up her napkin, wiped her mouth, and asked, "Ed, do you want the short version or the long?"

"The long version, of course," Ed said. Sasha smiled and said, "I'll even do it in your German so your parents can understand everything better."

Taking a deep breath, Sasha began. "That day I left, I pointed Copper to the west. After that, I didn't care where he went or how fast he went. He stayed at a nice, easy, slow gallop most of the day. Just after sunset, he stopped by a grove of trees that had a small stream running through it. I slid off, took the bags off his withers, got out my blanket, and sat down on it. I tried to eat a piece of jerky, but I just was not hungry. Copper went over to the stream, got a drink of water, and ate some grass until it was almost dark. Then he came and stood right beside where I was lying on the blanket. When he did that, I just couldn't help myself. I was so thankful you gave him to me I started to cry.

"Occasionally, Copper would nuzzle me like he was trying to say, 'It is okay, Sasha. Don't cry. I will stay right here all night.' I think I cried most of the night. I know I slept very little if any, and Copper was right beside me all night."

By this time, Katrina knew that Ed and Sasha were more than just good friends as Ed had introduced Sasha to her earlier, but she graciously listened to Sasha's intriguing story.

Sasha took a couple of forkfuls of mashed potatoes and some roast beef, picked up her napkin, wiped her mouth, and said, "This is such a delicious dinner!" Smiling, she continued her story. "The next morning, just after it got light, Copper went to the stream, drank some water, and ate grass until the sun came up. Then he came and waited for me to get my things back into the bags and placed them on his withers. I swung onto his back, and he continued at a slow, easy gallop in the same direction as the day before. I just let him go where he wanted.

"That evening, he stopped by a grove of trees again. But this time, there was a beautiful pond with crystal-clear water. After I got my stuff off him, he went to the pond to drink and continued to eat grass until just about dark. Then he walked over to me and stood where I was. Again, I just could not believe how smart and kind Copper was to me, and I started to cry again. Occasionally, he would nuzzle me like he was saying, 'Don't cry, Sasha. I'll stay right here by you all night.'"

At that point, Ed and most of the family had to wipe some tears from their eyes. Sasha took another couple of forkfuls of potatoes and roast beef. Then picked up her napkin, wiped her lips, and continued her story.

"The next morning, a while before sunup, Copper went to drink some water and grazed until about sunrise. When he finished, he came, stood by me, and waited for me to get ready to go. When I swung unto his back, again, he went in the same direction at a slow, easy gallop. I was beginning to wonder if he knew where we were going because I sure had no idea.

"That evening, about an hour before sundown, there were storm clouds in the west. Copper stopped by a grove of trees and just a small water hole. I guess he figured, 'Any port in a storm!'"

Everybody had to laugh at that. Sasha paused for a moment to eat a couple more forkfuls of her dinner and drank some water. She wiped her mouth with her napkin and continued her story.

"I really did not care anymore where we stayed for the night. I was so tired! I hadn't slept more than an hour or two in four nights. I slid off Copper, took my stuff off his withers, lay down, and immediately fell into a very deep sleep. I was so tired.

"Just about sundown, Copper was nickering and stomping his feet. I heard him, but I just could not make myself wake up. Finally, he pushed me with his nose and whinnied very loudly. That finally woke me up. I sat up and said, 'What is it, Copper? Can't you let me sleep when I am finally able to?' Again, he whinnied very loudly, shook his head, and stomped his feet.

"I noticed it was deathly still, no wind at all. I stood up and looked around. The sky looked purple! When I looked toward the southwest, there was a monster tornado out there, and I could tell it was headed right toward Copper and me. I did not pick up anything. I swung onto Copper's back and said, 'Go, Copper.' He took off to the northwest, and I have never seen him run so fast. I actually grabbed hold of his mane so I wouldn't fall off.

"In a few minutes, he slowed down to a walk, turned around, and we watched the tornado go by just where we had been. Copper had saved my life! We walked back to where I had been sleeping. There was nothing there. The tornado took everything I had, including those bags you loaned me, Ed." She paused and choked back tears.

"It's okay, Sasha. Don't worry about those bags. I can always make some more if I decide I need some."

She looked at him and said, "Like always, you're so kind to me." Sasha continued her story. "That night, I literally slept on the ground. I was so tired I could have slept anywhere. Copper actually had to wake me up by nuzzling me the next morning. But he was kind enough to wait until well after sunup before he woke me.

"Since the tornado took everything, I didn't have to pack anything the next morning. I didn't even have anything to eat or drink."

"When I swung onto Copper, he immediately took off in a different direction. As near as I could tell, we were going straight south. In less than half an hour, I could see a farm in the distance. Copper was headed toward the farm. When we arrived at the farm, the first thing I saw was this very handsome young man at the well, drawing water. Copper went directly to him. The young man looked at me, and in his native language, and mine, he asked, 'May I help you, miss?' I had not heard anybody speak that language in almost eleven years. I'm surprised that I could still understand it.

"I slid off Copper and went to him. I fell into his arms and started crying. I immediately knew I had found who I was looking for, someone like me. At the time, I did not know how much like me he was. He took me to the house. When I saw the people he was living with, I knew right away they were Mennonites. They looked just like the Regiers and the rest of the people I had been going to church with. Their names were Pete and Lena Stucky."

When Sasha said their names, all of Ed's family laughed and said almost in unison, "That's how you learned our German!"

Sasha giggled and said, "Yes, that is how I learned your German. They had six children, three girls and three boys, plus this wonderful guy beside me. And they still had room for me. They immediately told me I could stay with them as long as I wanted."

Sasha finished the food on her plate, wiped her mouth with the napkin, and said, "I have just a little more to tell you. You could probably guess that almost right away, Solu and I were drawn to each other. In fact, the Stuckys about had to chain us up at night to keep us apart." She looked at her handsome husband and saw he had a grin on his face and was nodding his head in agreement.

"Then about a month ago, a government man came to the house and asked Pete if he knew anything about the army raid on the Kancha village that was just a few miles from where they lived. Pete asked, 'Are you talking about the raid that happened about eleven years ago?'

"The government man said, 'Yes, that would be it.'

"Pete said, 'My wife and I have had the lone survivor of that raid living with us ever since. At the time, he was about five years old. His papa hid him under a pile of buffalo hides. We found him wandering around the village about three days after the raid. He was the only survivor.'

"The government man said, 'I'm sorry, sir. The army had a big misunderstanding. They were supposed to move the Kancha to the Indian Nations down in what is now called Oklahoma Territory, and place them on the reservation, not kill them. They did the same thing about a hundred miles east of here. I have heard one small girl survived that raid.'

"When the man said that, Pete said to Lena, 'Go get, Sasha. She can tell him her story.'

"I told the man how my mama lay on top of me and saved my life. The man said he had a lot of money to give to all the survivors of those two raids because the government was paying them retribution for the wrong that was done to their villages. 'Since you two are the only survivors, you get all the money.' He gave Solu and me $500.00 each.

"First, we are using the money to go to school in Newton to be schoolteachers. We want to teach native boys and girls the three Rs. We already have jobs waiting for us in Lame Deer, Montana. There is a school there that has not had a teacher for several years. The people there are the Northern Cheyenne."

Then Sasha said, "I want to say just one more thing. I will always be grateful to the Mennonites, especially the Regiers who took me in. They taught me about God, but Ed taught me to trust in God. When we were together, Ed always told me to trust in God. The last thing he told me before I rode away was, 'Sasha, trust in God.' That was all I could do when Copper was taking me away.

"Do you know God sent that tornado to take away everything I had and then I had no alternative but to trust in God? The morning after the tornado, Copper went south. We had always been going west. Copper knew I needed food and water, so he headed south where there was food and water, and something even better, a man from my own people waiting for me."

Mama got up and walked around the table to Sasha. She put her arms around her, kissed her on the cheek, and said, "That was such a touching story, Sasha, and thanks so much for telling it in our German. You speak it perfectly."

After they all finished eating, Solu and Sasha stayed and chatted for just a few minutes. They seemed excited to be moving clear to Montana in just a couple of years. They were confident that they would be accepted by those people, but they were not as sure if they could accept the cold Montana winters. Ed told Sasha that he knew her well enough that he was sure she could adapt to mostly anything that was thrown at her, and the Montana winters would be no exception.

Sasha then looked at Solu and said they should be going. He nodded his head and got up.

Sasha went to each member of Ed's family, hugged them, and said, "God bless you." To Katrina, after saying God bless you, she whispered something in her ear that brought a smile to her face. When she came to Ed, she said, "God bless you, Ed. I will never forget you. I can't give you a real kiss anymore, but I can sure kiss your hand."

Ed said, "I will never forget you, Sasha." He took her hand and kissed it.

Sasha and Solu walked out the door. Solu whistled at his horse, and he came trotting up to him. Sasha looked at Ed and mouthed to him, "Did you see that?" After Solu swung onto the back of his horse, Sasha grabbed his arm and swung on behind him.

Ed looked at Katrina. Her jaw had dropped as she looked at Ed and asked in astonishment, "How did she do that?"

The End

ABOUT THE AUTHOR

Keith grew up on a small farm in a Mennonite community in Central Kansas. He still lives in the same house, on the same farm where he grew up.

When Keith was twelve years old, his father bought a used combine and truck, and went to Oklahoma to do custom harvesting, that is, cut wheat for other farmers, to supplement his small farm income. At twelve years old, Keith drove the combine most of the time. He always says he was too young to do anything else. When Keith's father retired, Keith and his wife, Mary, took over the operation. They traveled from Oklahoma to South Dakota for thirty-seven years, harvesting wheat for other farmers, developing lifelong relationships with many of them since they returned year after year to harvest their wheat.

For many years, Keith wrote a daily journal of the harvesting operation. That added to his workload, but he found he enjoyed doing it, and he said that was what got him into writing.

When Keith and Mary retired from custom harvesting several years ago and stayed home all summer on their farm, Keith found he had more time on his hands than he knew what to do with. Not one to sit and do nothing, he started doing what he enjoyed doing, writing. He has written an autobiography, which is not yet published; and since romance is his favorite book to read, he decided to write one himself.

Keith and Mary are still active in the Mennonite church where Keith grew up. He teaches an adult Sunday school, and Mary works with the ladies' circle of the church.

CPSIA information can be obtained
at www.ICGtesting.com
Printed in the USA
LVHW010725290420
654635LV00006B/534

9 781098 026769